PAINTED MONSTERS
& OTHER STRANGE BEASTS

Other books by Orrin Grey

Anthologies:

Fungi (with Silvia Moreno-Garcia)

Chapbooks:

Gardinel's Real Estate (with M. S. Corley)
The Mysterious Flame

Collections:

Never Bet the Devil & Other Warnings

Praise for Orrin Grey's *Painted Monsters & Other Strange Beasts*

"*Painted Monsters & Other Strange Beasts* is a fantastic follow-up to Grey's first collection, *Never Bet the Devil*. This is the kind of writing that shows what can still be done with the classical weird."
 —Laird Barron, author of *The Beautiful Thing That Awaits Us All*

"The ghosts of old movie monsters stalk the pages of Orrin Grey's second collection. Here we find grave robbers and haunted houses side-by-side with vampires and kaiju. 'The Red Church' even features a serial killer who could have been taken (or is that sliced?) straight out of an Argento film. But it's the great German Expressionist F.W. Murnau whose influence is perhaps felt most keenly. In the title piece, *Nosferatu*'s Count Orlok is recast as a reclusive Mexican auteur, while Murnau's *Faust* provides the dramatic images which close out the eerily beautiful 'Night's Foul Bird.' Such haunting scenes recur throughout *Painted Monsters*, spaced together as closely as the stills on a film-strip and coaxed into motion by Grey's rapid-fire pacing. This is an outstanding collection, one to which you will return again and again long after the house lights have come up."
 —Daniel Mills, author of *The Lord Came at Twilight*

"The horror genre is a many-splintered thing. Grey collects those splinters, mixes and matches them, concocting a beast of a collection that is as fun as it is scary, as charming as it is chilling."
 —Philip Gelatt, writer of *Europa Report* and *Petrograd*, director of *The Bleeding House*

"In his latest collection, Orrin Grey not only pays homage to the classic horror films of yesteryear, he tears down the silver screen to reveal the true horrors that lurk on the other side. Fans of H. P. Lovecraft, Vincent Price, and the Hammer horror films will feel right at home."
 —Ian Rogers, author of *Every House Is Haunted*

Praise for Orrin Grey's *Painted Monsters & Other Strange Beasts*

"Orrin Grey's work specializes in old-school horror iconography—Universal monster movies, Roger Corman Poe adaptations, found footage epistolary narratives—run through a pop-culture blender set on frappé, and *Painted Monsters* (whose title derives from a quote from Peter Bogdanovich's *Targets*, with old Boris Karloff playing a version of himself while commenting on a version of his career) proves no exception to this rule. The result: inventive, assonant, literally dreadful. If you're looking for something between Ray Bradbury's headlong genre-bending fabulist glee and the *Insidious* movie franchise's unapologetic vaudeville creep, then Grey's your man."

—Gemma Files, author of *Experimental Film*

"Orrin Grey's roots (or should I say tentacles?) run deep, squeezing the best from horrors both classic and obscure, twisting them in his own particular way. He's a fine storyteller who'll pull you in, and so will *Painted Monsters*. Don't miss it!"

—Norman Partridge, author of *Dark Harvest*

PAINTED MONSTERS
& OTHER STRANGE BEASTS

ORRIN GREY

WORD HORDE
PETALUMA, CA

TABLE OF CONTENTS

For Vincent Price, Peter Cushing, Christopher Lee,
Boris Karloff, Bela Lugosi, Peter Lorre, and all the rest.
They don't make 'em like you anymore.

THE MONSTER GUY: AN INTRODUCTION TO ORRIN GREY

1. *Monster Awareness Month.* Late in 2010, Orrin Grey e-mailed me to ask if I'd be interested in participating in something called Monster Awareness Month. During the following March, Orrin and a handful of other writers would post appreciations of and reflections on various monster-related texts on a dedicated website. If I wanted to contribute something, Orrin wrote, they'd love to have me.

I did take part in Monster Awareness Month, with a short, autobiographical piece on my childhood viewing of a couple of B-movies. I was happy enough with my essay, but it was Orrin's contribution to the project that I found most impressive. In a lucid, thoughtful essay, he discussed the films of Guillermo del Toro, shuttling back and forth between the politicized phantasia of *Pan's Labyrinth* and the anarchic hero's journey of *Hellboy*. Critics often divide del Toro's movies into his more historically-rooted productions and his more adventure-oriented features, with the former receiving the lion's share of acclaim. Orrin bridged the gap between these kinds of films through the figure of the monster (which, for what it's worth, still seems to me the unifying concern in del Toro's work). In particular, Orrin highlighted del Toro as an artist in love with monsters, to such a degree that he felt compelled to do something interesting with them.

Afterwards, I would realize that this description might be applied to Orrin's creative work, as well.

2. *Marsupial Werewolves and Fried Alligator.* I first met Orrin Grey in May of 2011, at the World Horror Convention, which was being held in Austin. I'm sure we exchanged greetings at the con hotel, itself, but I didn't spend any substantial time with him until the second night of the convention, when I and a couple of friends ventured across the street from the hotel to an enormous restaurant specializing in Texas and southwestern cuisine. Sighting us at our table in the bar, Orrin waved for my friends and me to join him in the restaurant proper. He was seated with Joe Hill and Steve Niles, a plate of fried alligator on the table between them, dipping sauces to either side. After introductions were made, Orrin, Joe, and Steve returned to the serious business of listing and arguing the top ten werewolf movies ever made. I couldn't contribute much more than my appreciation for *An American Werewolf in London* and *Ginger Snaps*; the rest of the discussion left me far behind. At one point, the conversation moved to the third film in the *Howling* series, which is set in Australia and in which the werewolves have become marsupial. Orrin had a surprising amount to say about the virtues of the film.

It's tempting to make a joke of this, but I'm reminded instead of something Stephen King mentions in *Danse Macabre*, his informal study of the horror field. There is, King argues, genuine aesthetic pleasure to be found in a great many movies that might appear, at first glance, unpromising. Such enjoyment is an experience distinct from that of celebrating camp. In embracing camp, the viewer takes pleasure in the failures of a film and, really, in their ability to transgress accepted norms of taste and merit. What King describes is the ability to recognize a film's successes, its moments of integrity, whether of character, plot, or theme, through the fog of those elements that don't work. You might call it the experience of the aficionado, and it arises from an understanding and appreciation of the way a specific kind of film works, its traditions and tropes. King compares it to the ability of some experts to tap a glass and know from the resulting sound if it's cheap glass or priceless crystal. It's a gift in short supply. I believe Orrin demonstrated it, between bites of alligator.

3. *Fungal Reading.* The next time Orrin invited me to contribute to a project, it was an anthology he and Silvia Moreno-Garcia were co-editing. Titled *Fungi,* it was to feature stories in which the eponymous organism played a central role. Knowing their prospective contributors, Orrin and Silvia cautioned against heading directly for the Cordyceps option (that's the so-called "zombie fungus" that colonizes the brains of insects and turns them into its vehicles). We might wish to consider some of the previous uses to which writers and filmmakers had put the fungus. There was, of course, Jeff VanderMeer, whose *Ambergris* stories and novels run riot with fungal organisms and technology. But there was also William Hope Hodgson's story, "The Voice in the Night," and its film adaptation by Japanese director Ishiro Honda, *Matango* (aka *Attack of the Mushroom People* aka *Fungus of Terror*). Those who wanted to range even further afield could have a look at Stephen King's "Grey Matter" or Brian Lumley's "Fruiting Bodies." Who knew? I thought.

Of course, the answer was, Orrin.

4. *From Goethe to Barron (to Grey).* Unsurprisingly, Orrin Grey's fiction is full of monsters. It's also no surprise that his stories display an awareness of the traditions in which he's working, deftly moving between popular image and literary incarnation. Take the figure of the witch, which is at the center of his excellent story, "Walpurgisnacht," his contribution to Ross E. Lockhart and Justin

Steele's *The Children of Old Leech: A Tribute to the Carnivorous Cosmos of Laird Barron*. The story is full of allusions to the world of Laird Barron's fiction, from the lost films of Eadweard Muybridge to the Black Ram Lodge. It also echoes the plot dynamics of some of Barron's stories, focusing on a couple whose relationship is starting to fray, leaving them vulnerable to unholy forces. At the same time, as its title indicates, the story alludes to the scene of the Witches' Sabbath in Goethe's *Faust Part 1*. In so doing, the narrative draws a line between Goethe and Barron's uses of the witch. In addition, the story makes implicit reference to James Hogg's *Confessions of a Justified Sinner*, and explicit reference to Goya's art, specifically his Black Paintings. The story offers a perfect symbol for the relation between past and present art in its description of the *Sender Brocken*, a pair of towers, one old, one new, one a hotel, the other a great antenna. (Needless to say, the image also evokes the interchange between Barron's fiction and Orrin's.) In the hands of a less-skilled writer, so elaborate a narrative construction might collapse under the weight of its own ambitions. But Orrin avoids this fate by building his story around a sympathetically-drawn protagonist, whose struggle to understand the events unfolding around him lends the story resonance. The result is a narrative that succeeds on its own terms, even as it pays tribute to Laird Barron's work.

In this regard, "Walpurgisnacht" is typical of the stories assembled in this, Orrin Grey's second collection. With a sure hand, Orrin brings elements gathered from his extensive, appreciative knowledge of the horror tradition together with compellingly-drawn characters to craft stories whose effects linger long after their final lines. The word *monster*, etymology tells us, refers to that which is shown. What is shown in these stories is the talent of their author. Orrin Grey is a monster: watch him.

—John Langan

"My kind of horror is not horror anymore.
No one's afraid of a painted monster."
— *Targets* (1968)

THE WORM THAT GNAWS

I've 'ad loadsa bad jobs in my day, but this un's the worst by a mile. Trompin' around in the boneyards at midnight, diggin' up dead folks wi' a wooden spade, breakin' open the caskets wi' a mattock, an 'aulin' 'em up an out by the 'eads. Christ.

The mist creeps up 'til it's so thick ya can't 'ardly see the groun' for it, makes the tombstones look like ships at sea where they thrust up outta it. Cold as a witch's tit, an only one bottle between us, Wolfe an I.

'Course it's illegal. I ain't 'ad but a job or two that weren't, in one way or t'other. But the fines ain't steep, an the constables tend ta look t'other way. 'Sides, the pay's worth the risks. Good pay, for a fella like me, or a fella like Wolfe.

'E's the boss, is Wolfe. Been at the game a long time, compared ta me, an 'e ain't like ta let me forget it. Big fella, shaped like a barrel, face all red an puffy from too much drink. "You'd drink too, if ya'd seen what I seen," 'e always tells me, as if I don't drink.

Knows 'is business, though, give 'im that. 'Ere we are, at the grave. Anna Fairchild. Pretty name. Wonder if she's pretty? Wonder if she'll still be pretty, when we get down to 'er? Won't be after, that's for sure. We'll push Wolfe's big metal hook—like a fishhook fer catchin' whales—up unner 'er chin, inta the soft stuff there an through 'er jaw, then both of us'll get on the rope, 'aulin' 'er up. Girls is best, 'cause they're light.

7

No, she prob'ly won' be pretty after all that. An if she is, she won't be when the sods at the anatomy school get done 'ackin' 'er up.

Still, she's dead an I ain't. She don't got no cares, an me, cares is all I got. That's the way a the world.

Wolfe loosens up the sod, an now I'm diggin'. 'Ate this bloody spade, 'ate this bloody weather. Least it ain't rainin'. Cloudy. Cold. But no sign a rain. Thank Christ fer small favors.

Fella with a skull for a 'ead over there watchin' me, lookin' down on me like 'e knows what I'm doin' an 'e don't approve. Why would ya want a great big statue a Death right there on yer tombstone, remindin' everybody what come ta visit ya, I dunno. Damn waste a money, is what it is! The whole thing: fancy caskets an tombstones an statues. The dead don't care. They don't know the difference between this place an the operatin' table.

I don't want no damn tombstone when I die. A good thing, too, cause I ain't like ta 'ave one. I could 'aul corpses outta the ground from 'ere 'til Judgement Day an not 'ave enough coin for a monument like Ol' Skull-Head there.

Naw, when I'm dead let the anatomy classes 'ave me. Let 'em cut me up an parcel me out ta the students. Marcus gets the upper torso, Robert gets the right 'and, Louis gets the left, an Peter can 'ave the 'ead this time. Let me make a few shillings for some other Resurrection Man ta waste on whiskey an girls.

Wolfe says it's 'cause I'm young that I ain't worried about death. "The older ya get," 'e says, "the more scared ya get a dyin', an the less scared ya get a everythin' else."

The sound a the spade on the casket is 'ollow, like somebody rappin' on the door wi' their cane. 'S lonely like that, too. Makes ya think about tree branches tappin' against the window at night, an all the scary stories ya got told when ya were little. Mostly, though, it just makes ya wanna get the damn job done.

Wolfe always puffs up like a bantam rooster before 'e swings the mattock. 'E looks like a right arse, but 'e's good an in a coupla swings 'e's got a 'ole cleared an we can see Miss Fairchild's 'ead.

'Cept... Bugger me, it's just a skull. Did we get the wrong grave? We ain't never got the wrong grave before.

Wolfe's light on the 'eadstone. Anna Fairchild. 'Course it is, 'cause I read the name on the damn thing once already, didn't I?

Mary Mother a God, somethin' *moved* in there! Wolfe's still got the light on the 'eadstone, so I grab 'is arm an push it down.

She sure ain't pretty no more. An she sure as hell ain't movin'. But somethin' is. There, I see it again, *inside* the skull.

Worms! Oh bloody 'ell, the casket's full a worms!

***

Goin' back empty's always bad for business. The schools rely on us for bodies, an if we can't supply 'em they'll find some other blokes who will. Plenty of folks around wi' more bills than scruples. Wolfe an I don't pretend we're anythin' special.

'Course, we didn't really 'ave much choice. Not enough time to pick out another body, an what were we suppose ta do, bring 'em a skeleton an a bunch a worms? Doubt they'd wanna give up their shillings for that.

Wolfe's seen a lot more a life—an death—than I 'ave. I ask 'im, 'as 'e ever seen anythin' like that before. 'E just shakes 'is 'ead. "No," 'e says, an again, "No."

***

Resurrection men. I don't know who first started callin' us that, us or them. I don't know 'ow many of us there is. Don't really think of us as an "us." There's just me an Wolfe. We seen some other blokes, but we try ta stay outta their way, an if they know what's good for 'em they stay outta ours.

We got a 'andful a places we go. Lonesome places, mostly, where the constables don't. Ya'd think they'd catch us, since we keep comin' back, but they don't care. Only worry we got is a 'usband or a fiancé waitin' up wi' a pistol, an we watch out fer that.

We keep comin' back 'ere, though, more than the others. The best diggin's 'ere, like a mine that keeps payin' out. Or it was. Since Anna Fairchild we aint 'ad much luck wi' this place.

Christ, I still remember 'er name.

Third time we been back since then, third time we dug 'em up. Nothin' left a the bodies, just worms an bones. Jesus, 'ow do they eat 'em so fast? They gotta get through the casket first, don't they? An this one ain't been in the ground a day. What we gotta do, take 'em off the wagon?

There's blokes that kill to fill the tables at the anatomy schools. I know it as well as anyone. Folks at the schools know it too, though they pretend they don't. But I ain't interested in stretching me neck fer a few pounds.

We didn't talk about it, but I guess Wolfe an I both knew we was comin' out 'ere early tonight 'cause we might 'ave ta dig twice. 'Cause, without sayin' anythin', I just go over an start diggin'. An older grave, the body won't be worth much ta the schools, but I got to know.

Thunk! An then the mattock, almost 'fore I can get outta the way. 'S a man, or was, though I dunno 'ow I can tell. The features're gone, just starin' sockets an blank white bones an the worms, pale an squirmin' like a bed all 'round 'im.

Wolfe dropped the lantern, I guess. 'S out, anyway. Glad there's a moon tonight, though usually's a bane ta such as us. Thanks ta it I can see Wolfe run over ta another grave an start 'ackin' at it wi' the mattock, throwin' bits a dirt out behind like a hound diggin' for a bone.

There's the sound a the mattock splinterin' the casket, an then there's Wolfe retchin' an cursin', but I don't 'ave ta go an look ta know what 'e's found.

***

"Know 'ow I got inta this business?" Wolfe asks me at the pub. That's 'is what? Fifth? "I were married once, y'know?"

'Ard to see Wolfe as married, but 'e 'olds up 'is fingers an there it is—years gone now an almost lost unner a film a graveyard dirt—the lighter circle 'round 'is finger where the weddin' ring use'ta sit. "'Ad me an honest job—well, more honest anyway. 'Ad me a place, though it weren't much. 'Ad me a woman ta come 'ome to ev'ry night. Pretty thing, too, though you'd not think it ta see 'er now, I wager."

'E ain't lookin' at me, thank God. If 'e did, 'e'd see I'm near ta squirmin' in my seat. Wolfe don't talk like this, ain't never talked like this, an 'e's makin' me mighty nervous doin' it now.

"We was young, I guess," 'e says. "She was, an I know if I weren't young then I felt it. Yer stupid when yer young, an that's good. Maybe yer still young enough ta be stupid like that, ya find the right girl. Ya think things is always gonna get better. Not all at once, but gradual. On balance. Ya ever felt like that?"

'E takes a drink, but don't wait fer me ta answer, an I'm glad 'cause if I answered it'd be "no" an I think that'd stop 'is story. An while the story's makin' me uncomfortable, the silence'd be worse.

"'Course, it don't. Maybe for some folks it does. I use'ta think so, now I know better'n ta think about it at all. What matters 's that it didn't fer me, an it didn't fer 'er. I lost me job's 'ow it started. She took it better'n I did, an that's good 'cause I didn't take it s'well. Then, one mornin', she's comin' back ta our place an she falls in front of a carriage. Somehow er other she'd gotten ahold a some eggs. She was gonna make 'em fer me breakfast, I guess. There they was, I remember, eggs all over the road, an all of 'em busted."

'E finishes 'is drink. I don't blame 'im, an I do the same, partly 'cause I need it an partly ta keep from 'avin' ta say anythin'.

"I sold 'er body to the resurrection man," 'e says, quickly now. "What did I care, eh? An most a 'er were intact, in spite a the 'orses. I sold me ring. It was that or starve, eh?"

Christ, the thump a 'is bottle on the table makes me jump. "If I don't get to bury 'er, 'ave a place to go an leave the flowers, then why should other folks, eh? They can cut 'er up, they can cut up anybody. Jus' bodies anyway. Jus' meat. A man 'as ta make a livin', while 'e's alive. An ain't no bloody worms gonna beat me to it."

***

I think maybe Wolfe's gone crazy. So then why'm I goin' along? 'Cause we're partners, I guess.

The stuff in the wagon clinks together an sloshes. Sounds like we're 'aulin' liquor. God, I wish we was 'aulin' liquor.

I tried ta talk 'im inta givin' it up, inta goin' ta on a the other boneyards. We only found the worms in this one, but it were our best one, 'an 'e were 'avin' none a it. Wouldn't be beaten, 'e said. Not by worms.

'Srainin', of course. Be a blessin' 'cause it'll keep us from bein' seen. Be a curse if we was diggin', but we ain't, not tonight, though we got the mattock an the spade with us outta 'abit.

Wolfe says the rain'll be good, keep the fumes from gettin' too bad, though we got our bandanas up over our mouths, like high-waymen.

Fumes, I say. *Christ Jesus.* But 'e won't be dissuaded.

I don't know where 'e got the stuff. Said 'e 'ad a friend at one a the schools what owed 'im a favor.

Some favor! Fifteen bottles a carbolic. Fifteen! Like bottles a whiskey back there—clink clink—'cept they got labels on 'em says they're poison an then some.

The rain's let up a bit. Jus' drippin' off things now, like 'eavy fog. I 'ate the rain, even if it does keep the smell down. I 'ate the way it makes the trees look soggy, like they'd give if ya put yer 'and on 'em.

This is the grave we'd a dug up tonight, I guess, if we'd been dig-gin'. Just thinkin' 'bout all those worms down there. Rain's made the ground soft so it squishes under me boots, makes it easy to imagine 'em comin' up. Water's runnin' in rivulets down the 'ill, slidin' like snakes off the 'eadstones, so it looks like the ground's crawlin' an writhin' like it's made a worms.

There goes the tarp, an Wolfe's got a bottle an 'e's showin' me 'ow ta pour it, like I don't know 'ow ta pour somethin' onta the ground.

'E wasn' kiddin' 'bout the fumes, I guess. They rise up like smoke, yella an sick lookin' in the light from the lantern. I'm imaginin' what the grass'll look like tomorra or the day after or the day after that: yella an brittle an dead. Maybe tha's 'ow it ought ta be. Maybe all the grass an trees in a graveyard ought ta be dead. A reminder, like Ol' Skull-Head.

I see if I can spot the statue that was standin' near Anna Fairchild's grave. Anythin' ta stop lookin' at the ground an the poison fog that's comin' up as Wolfe pours the carbolic. But everythin' outside the little spot a light's a shadow, an all the monuments jus' look like black shapes crowdin' up on us. Patient brigands, waitin' 'til we're dead an gone. Like the anatomy students; like the worms.

Speak a the devil an 'e will appear, as my pa used ta say 'fore I ran off from 'ome. They're boilin' up outta the ground, writhin' an squirmin' as the acid burns 'em. An Jesus, the sound it makes. Sounds like they're screamin', an Wolfe's laughter ain't no better. 'E don't sound triumphant, like I think 'e means ta, 'e just sounds crazy.

Wha's that? A shape outside the light? Constable, maybe, or, God 'elp us, a mourner? We weren't careful tonight like we shoulda been. Oh, tonight of all nights don't let it be a mourner.

But it ain't. Oh merciful 'eaven it ain't an I wish it was. The wind's up now, an the sackcloth is blowin' in black tatters 'round it, makin' it writhe like the worms. Only that ain't all sackcloth.

I got the spade, been 'oldin' it this whole time, an I hit it an knock pieces off that disappear, squirmin', inta the dark. Jesus Christ, Wolfe, get the lantern off it! I don't wanna see!

But I do see. There's bones under all those worms. Bones up an walkin' round like they got a new skin.

The sound that Wolfe makes I ain't got a name for, an 'e dashes the bottle a carbolic in its face, if it's got a face, an it's shrieking.

I'm runnin', I realize. The ground's wet an soft an I'm fallin' runnin' fallin' runnin' again. I ain't got the spade anymore. I ain't got nothin'.

Wolfe's beside me, an then 'e slips an goes down an doesn't get back up. I stop, stumble, look back. I'm gonna 'elp 'im, I know I am, but 'e comes up all covered in worms an behind 'im is the shadow of that thing, like Ol' Skull-Head, grinnin' an grinnin' outta a hood a worms an I don't 'elp 'im. I just run.

***

The rain's started ta come 'ard again. I feel it against the door at me back. I don't remember slidin' down 'ere, but I guess I did 'cause 'ere I am.

The door's locked. I remember doin' that, but I check again anyway, reachin' up wi' me 'and. I take it down, then I dunno, so I check again, an again.

I didn't see nothin'. Didn't see nothin', jus' a statue an some worms an it was dark an Wolfe an... Jesus Jesus *Jesus*.

A knock. Oh Christ, a knock on the door, soft but firm, like a rotten log. Just the rain. Just a gust a wind. Scarin' myself, all I'm doin'.

Again. There it is *again*.

"Charlie."

That's Wolfe's voice. 'E made it back. But it sounds as if 'e's 'urt, maybe. Talkin' through a mouthful a blood an broken teeth.

"Let me in, Charlie."

It must be awful bad. Sounds like a kid talkin' wi' 'is mouth fulla porridge.

I ain't gonna open the door. I'm gonna stay right 'ere an it'll go away. Oh Jesus, please let it go away. I'll do better. I won't be a resurrection man no more.

I don't care if the anatomy schools get me when I'm gone, but not this. Please not this.

"Let us in, Charlie."

I ain't gonna open the door, 'cause it ain't Wolfe. It'll look like 'im, right enough, least a little bit. Like someone wearin' 'is clothes, maybe, an a suit as 'is skin an a mask as 'is face. Not some-*one*, though. Some*thing*.

Worms. 'E'll be made a worms.

AUTHOR'S NOTES:

While "The Worm That Gnaws" may get its title and the idea for its monster from my favorite Lovecraft quote, it was written as an ode to all those grave robber duos who used to provide comic relief in the old black-and-white horror movies of the '30s. It was partly an exercise to see if I could write in that thick Edinburgh grave robber accent, and partly just an extension of my lasting obsession with cemeteries and resurrection men. The statue of Ol' Skull-Head is a nod to the grave robbing scene in James Whale's 1931 version of *Frankenstein*.

"The Worm That Gnaws" is the oldest story in this collection, and this is its first time in print, though it's been out in the world since 2009, when it was my first sale to *Pseudopod*. I struck up a pretty good relationship with them, and I've since sold two other stories to current *Pseudopod* editor Shawn Garrett. This is the only story I ever sold to them that wasn't a reprint. I figured it would work nicely in audio form, because of the accent, and I was more right than I could have guessed. Ian Stuart nailed the voice so perfectly that the podcast remains my preferred version of the story, and a favorite among *Pseudopod* listeners. If you enjoyed it here (or even if you didn't), I'd definitely recommend giving the podcast a listen.

When he bought the story, then-editor Ben Phillips said that it had "more apostrophes than any story I've ever seen." I'd imagine it probably still holds that record.

THE WHITE PRINCE

A
t night, then, it came crawling through Miss Anna's open window. A pale thing. I doubt it ever had seen the sun.

Why did she accept its embrace and not my own? By the time we knew the truth, she was already far gone, and her shame sealed her torn lips with silence. Neither would she speak to me, one of her suitors, nor to Peter, her fiancé. Visiting Dr. von Stane attended her that last night. Afterward, he pulled me aside and told me that, delirious, she pleaded for her "alabaster prince."

That final night we all waited: Peter crouched in her wardrobe, the rest of us in the next room. Lights hooded, hands sweating on the hafts of spears cut from the ash trees found down by the stream, listening for the sounds of its ascent. I thought I heard a wet sound, as if something damp slapped at the walls of the manor. We had to wait to be sure, wait until we saw the hideous outline set against the moonlight streaming through the open window, until it had slumped into the room and was almost upon her bed, as it had been now for how many nights. Only then did we reveal our lanterns and spring into the room.

Its bulbous eyes grew wide, swiveling in a batrachian face, as it peered at us. It was Peter who drove in the spear, piercing the damp, fleshy bag of the thing's body. It made a sound, not quite a dog's bark, and it stumbled back, its long fingers with their sucking pads reaching feebly for my friend, who drew away in terror.

The ungainly creature flopped for a moment, then disappeared out the window.

The gardener was the first to the ground, and found the spot where the body had fallen, the grass crushed flat and smeared with blood. Even in the dark we could see the trail it left, spatters of crimson that showed black in the lantern light. Peter's father, Sir Godfrey, organized the party to hunt it down. Peter wanted to go, demanded to go, but Dr. von Stane laid his hand on Peter's arm and said, "Anna needs you here, now more than ever," and so Peter stayed behind.

The good doctor, Sir Godfrey and I went out, along with the gardener and two of the stablehands. We armed ourselves with lanterns and spears, shotguns and revolvers, though I don't know if any of us really believed that the guns would do us much good against our quarry. Sir Godfrey brought along the hatchet from the woodpile behind the house.

We followed the trail into the woods that bordered the property, past a stream where the rocks were spattered with blood. One of the stablehands said something about how it "couldnae a got far, leakin' like that," but I thought of how bloated it had been, and wondered how much blood it could keep in that sack-like body, how much it could do without.

During the whole affair, no one had ever uttered the word "vampyre," not even Dr. von Stane, who told us to cut the branches from only the ash and sharpen them into long stakes. But all of us had read Mr. Stoker's work published the prior year and I doubt I was alone in my thinking. But then, was it really blood it took from frail Anna, those nights when it oozed into her bed? I had been the one who caught them together, I in my bold—dare I even admit, untoward—mission to change her mind about marrying Peter. I had seen it atop her, seen her hands caressing its clammy flesh. Certainly, though, it was taking *something* from her, for she had been wasting away before our very eyes, dying in front of us even as her countenance took on the glow of a girl newly in love.

As we trudged after the wounded creature through the dew-wet undergrowth of the forest, I knew that Anna would be dead before we returned. I had seen it in Dr. von Stane's eyes as we left. We were too late to save her, and now we were simply executioners, carrying out a sentence.

***

We found the cave among the moss-grown ruins of a monastery that had long since fallen to scattered stones. "Good Lord," Sir Godfrey said as we stood in a semicircle around the dark opening, scarcely larger than a pantry door. "I used to play near here when I was a boy. There were stories, but none of us believed..." His words died with a sigh.

One by one we crept into the dank, dripping tunnel, which seemed half-natural, though here and there hewn stones showed old carvings of monks with their heads bowed in prayer. We kept our spears before us, and our guns near at hand, moving like men hunting a bear, though what we found was something already half-dead, collapsed upon some ancient crypt, its moist skin heaving as it struggled to breathe. For all its inhumanity, it looked less a hideous supernatural creature, and more just a dying animal, but our disgust and pity were worse than our fear, and it was only a moment before one of the stablehands drove in his spear once, and then again. Sir Godfrey followed suit, and I stood and held the lantern aloft so they could see to do their grisly work.

As the thing died, it reached up and its spidery fingers found my wrist. I trembled, as if in forbidden pleasure, and saw not the ghastly creature I had seen before, but a youth, pale and frightened, his eyes shining with unshed tears. "Please," he said, his voice cracking, "please help me." Then Sir Godfrey brought down the hatchet, and severed his head.

I didn't speak to the others of what I had seen, but I urged them to carry the body impaled on their spears and not to touch it. We burned the remains on a pyre in the back garden, but only after Dr. von Stane had examined them carefully. He suggested that the creature must have exuded a toxin from its beslimed skin, perhaps a hallucinogen, like certain mushrooms. I thought of the boy I had seen, and remembered the fairy tale that we were all told as children, of the princess who kisses the frog and finds him transformed into a handsome prince. I watched the fire burn, and I shuddered.

AUTHOR'S NOTES:

"The White Prince" was written for Steve Berman's incubus anthology *Handsome Devil*, and it's one of a pair of stories that I wrote back-to-back exploring different takes on early portrayals of vampires in popular media. This one uses Stoker's *Dracula* as its jumping-off point, of course, and the many-angled romances that always sat at the hearts of those early vampire tales, but it also plays with the vampire's seductive hypnotic abilities. I was originally going to call it "The Frog Prince," but Steve felt like that gave the game away a bit too early.

NIGHT'S FOUL BIRD

The Arcangel Hotel is six stories tall. We live on the top floor, Mother and I. The man on the other side keeps pigeons on the roof, all lined up in wire cages. He says that he's taught them how to do tricks, that he used to perform with them on the stage, but all I've ever seen him do is take them out to feed them. He holds them in his hand, their legs gripped between his thumb and forefinger. He showed me how and I held one. It felt warm and fluttery in my palm, even when it wasn't moving, and I could feel the blood churning through it. It was like holding a living heart. I remember thinking that next to birds, people must seem to already be dead.

The man's name is Steiner, but I call him "Mr. Birdman." He also has a parrot. A cockatoo, he says it is. Big and champagne pink, its feathers as soft as silk scarves. I'm always surprised when I touch feathers. I expect them to feel one way and they always feel another. Soft as the petals of a flower when I think they'll be stiff, rigid like the tiny bones of a fish when I expect them to be soft.

Mr. Birdman's cockatoo is huge, almost as big as my torso. It has a black beak and shiny black-button eyes. It knows how to talk a little, but I've only ever heard it say, "Hello," which it stretches out so that it comes out sounding like "hollow."

Mother says I oughtn't to fool around with Mr. Birdman's pigeons or his cockatoo—which is named "Shirley." She says that

birds are filthy creatures and she doesn't know why such an otherwise refined-seeming man would truck with them. She says that
pigeons, in particular, carry disease. Like rats.

Mother doesn't seem to like or do or approve of much, ever since
Father "died." Died is what I have to say he did if anyone asks,
but really, he left. I know that he isn't dead, because I got a letter
from him once. It had my name on it, and our address here at the
Arcangel Hotel, but Mother got it first and never let me read it,
so I've had to imagine what it must have said. Sometimes, I think
that he was apologizing because he was called away to some noble
quest, or because he was the target of a secret society and could not
endanger our lives by staying. Sometimes, he has a new wife and a
new family, and he is inviting me to come live with him.

I don't think that I would go, though, even if that was what the
letter said. I'd feel bad leaving Mother behind, and Mr. Birdman,
and the city is the only place I've ever known.

On Friday nights, I take some money from out of the bowl in
the living room and I go down the street to the theater. There, I
sit in the dark and watch the moving pictures. Mother doesn't approve of them, either, but she's never been to one. I tell her they're
like magic and she tells me there's no such thing.

Really, though, I don't try very hard to convince her. I'm glad
that she doesn't go to the theater with me. While she already
doesn't approve of me going, she certainly wouldn't approve of
the ones I like best. They come from Germany, big and grim and
foreboding. Murnau and Wiene and Leni. One day, I watched
Nosferatu, and I lay awake all night afterward, imagining the moment when Count Orlok rises up from his coffin, stiff as a board.
Terrified, yes, by every creak and flutter, but something else, too.
Alive, illuminated. I could feel the beating of my heart, feel the
rush and heat of blood in my veins. I felt as if I were glowing in
the dark, as if I were giving off light.

***

Last week, a man moved into the building. He lives in the same rooms as us but on the fourth floor rather than the sixth. On the floor between is a plump-cheeked lady whose two sons both died in the War. I call her the "Widow Flowers," because she is always drying flowers in the kitchen above her sink. She gives them out to everyone as gifts at every relevant occasion. I wonder if she loves them because they're beautiful but already dead, unchanging, like a photograph, but Mother says I mustn't ask people such questions.

The new man is strange, pallid and sunken, and his head seems to taper from top to bottom, as though his chin is forming like a stalactite from his face. His eyes are very pale and he has an odd way of staring at you as if he's actually looking at whatever's just behind you, instead. Mother says that he's sweet and that I mustn't judge. That many of the young men who came back from the War came back just like him. I don't think he seems young, but Mother says that he's not much older than me. She blames the War for that, too.

He says his name is "Milton," but in my mind, I'm already calling him "Mr. Chaney," because there's something about him that reminds me of Lon Chaney's faux-vampire in *London After Midnight*, which I loved up 'til the end. Maybe it's his long coat, which he wears always draped over his shoulders, his arms not through the sleeves. Maybe it's his shadow, which seems to cling too close to him, to hunch at his back when he stands near walls, as though it's whispering secrets in his ears.

Mother says that I'm sensitive, but that I should keep it to myself, and that I mustn't judge people until they've given me a reason to, as it says in the Bible. I don't think that *is* what it says in the Bible, but I don't contradict her.

***

Mother wants me to get to know Mr. Chaney better. She even suggested that he could "take you to one of those moving picture shows that you're so fond of." And when my reaction was less than she'd hoped, she added, "It's really not right for a young lady of your age to go unattended."

Mother seems to like Mr. Chaney and seems to think that I should, too, but he makes me uncomfortable. When she introduced us the first time, the hand that he clasped mine in was as smooth and hard as the keys of a piano, and when he raised my hand to his lips, his breath was hot.

I watch him sometimes, when he goes out. Mother says he works at night, at a factory somewhere, but she doesn't say which one or what he does. Mother says that everyone in the building likes him, that he's a charming young man, but I watch him when he goes out at night, and I see that whatever side of the street he walks down is always deserted. If there's a couple out taking a stroll, they always cross to the other side, even if they are blocks away, even if they haven't seen him yet, even if their eyes are only for each other. They do it without even knowing. If you asked them why, they couldn't tell you. If they met Mr. Chaney, they'd like him. They'd say that he's a nice young man, just as Mother does. They certainly wouldn't cross the street to avoid him, not on purpose, but they do it anyway. They just know to without knowing why, the same way that birds know to flock together.

***

The Widow Flowers is the first to go. They find her in the little backyard behind the hotel, where the men stand and smoke, sometimes. Her throat is cut and there's a spray of flowers, fresh flowers, tucked into her blouse.

There are more fresh flowers at her funeral, white lilies and other things. It seems wrong to me, as if the people at the funeral didn't know her, what few people there are. The smell of them seems overpoweringly strong in the little church, but Mother says that we have to go because we were her neighbors and she had no one else. Mother and I go into her rooms, too, and help box up her personal things. There are flowers still drying above the sink. On her dressing table, I find photographs of her two sons in their Army uniforms, frozen forever in that moment just before death.

They clear out all of her things. Some are shipped off to distant relatives, but the dried flowers are thrown in the trash bin behind the hotel. I can see them out the back window, the one in the kitchen. I stand there sometimes in the early morning and look out. I can see part of the backyard where the Widow Flowers was found and I can see the sun rise through a space between two buildings. Sometimes, Mr. Chaney stands out there just before dawn, when he gets home from the factory or wherever he goes at night, and smokes a cigarette while watching that space between the buildings fill up with light. He always goes in before the sun peeks through. I hope he never looks up and, if he does, I hope he never sees me standing in the window.

***

Now there is an empty space between our rooms and Mr. Chaney's. I can feel it there, in a way that I couldn't before when the Widow Flowers was in it, cooking and sleeping and drying her flowers. I feel it all the time, hollow and lifeless, dark and silent, the shades drawn down, dust slowly settling on the floors and the counters. It feels cold and it aches, like a cavity in a tooth. And worse, it provides no buffer. Though there are still the same walls and floors and ceilings, still the same distance, I feel there's nothing to separate our rooms from Mr. Chaney's any longer. I feel as if he's right beneath me, all the time. At night, when I'm in bed, it's as if he's lying underneath, pressed up against the bottom of my mattress. I dream that his arm comes up through the floorboards — not breaking them, just passing through, as if they aren't there, or as if he's a part of them — the nails on his hand suddenly sharp, suddenly long.

I wake with a start and sit up in bed. I have to put my own hand in my mouth and bite down so I don't scream. I don't look under the bed. If he is down there, I don't want to know.

Outside, snow has begun to fall.

***

I haven't been to the theater since the Widow Flowers died. Mother says that it's too dangerous, that she doesn't want me going out unless she knows where I'm going. I don't try to tell her that she knows where I'm going if I go to the theater. I don't want to argue.

Besides, ever since the snow started, no one seems to be going anywhere, anyway. The snow never stops. It piles up against the sides of the buildings, drifting doors closed and creeping up to the sills of windows. It's almost as dark during the days as it is at night and everything outside seems very far away. We are alone.

The next of us to die is a man downstairs. I had no name for him, because I rarely saw him. He dies in his rooms. They say he slit his wrists. He had a grown daughter who lived somewhere else in the city, and who would sometimes visit him with a golden-haired little son in tow. She comes to his rooms to gather his things so that Mother and I don't have to. I sit at the top of the stairs, and listen to her putting things into boxes and weeping softly. No one from the building goes to his funeral. I don't know if there were lilies.

After his daughter is gone, I go downstairs and find that his door is closed but not locked. I go in. The room is dim and empty. More than just unoccupied. I can tell somehow that no one lives there, anymore.

I walk around, touch my fingertips to the furniture, press down on the bed. There is nothing left to show that this was where a person had lived, had died, but I find a button on the floor, partially under the rug. A big silver button, like the ones on Mr. Chaney's coat.

***

At night, I lie on the floor of my bedroom and press my ear to the cold floorboards. I can hear Mr. Chaney in his room, pacing and reciting little snippets of poetry. It's always the same poem, one by Robert Blair that I've read before, and it does not reassure me.

"Doors creak," he mutters, "and windows clap, and night's foul bird rook'd in the spire screams loud." When I read them, I loved these words. I'd memorized them myself, or very near. They felt to me the way the films I watched felt, that pleasing shiver up my spine. Now, though, hearing them up through my floorboards, they are something else. "The Grave gainsays the smooth-complexion'd flatt'ry, and with blunt truth acquaints us what we are."

The week after the man downstairs died, I go over to Mr. Birdman's room and knock on his door, but I receive no answer save for a muffled "hollow" from Shirley. I know that he probably braved the snow for groceries or some other errand, but something makes me take the stairs up to the roof. I can barely push the roof door open past the snow that has piled up since it was opened last, which couldn't have been long before, because I find Mr. Birdman there, kneeling amidst a blizzard of snow and feathers, weeping, broken, his face in his hands. The wire boxes around him are all torn and shattered, and the bodies of the pigeons lie here and there, the blood poppy-bright against the white of the snow.

***

I can hear Mother in the other room, rocking and looking out the window at the darkness, at the night. It's been another week since I found Mr. Birdman and his pigeons and I haven't seen anyone from the building in all that time, only heard Mother rocking and Mr. Chaney pacing and reciting his verses. Outside, the streets are silent, filled with snow. No one passes, and the only lights are distant and hidden by the gloom.

I know that we're the only ones left in the building. I know it, the same way I've known so many things that Mother tells me I mustn't repeat nor act upon, even if they're right. If I put my hand to the wall, I can feel the building, feel the emptiness of all the rooms. I can feel it *waiting*, holding its breath.

I stand in the living room, watching Mother, who doesn't look away from the window, doesn't look at me. I go out onto the landing, to the top of the stairs. Across the hall, Mr. Birdman's door is ajar, and light spills out from inside. I could go push it open, could look inside, but there's no need. I already know what I would see. I can see it now, if I close my eyes. A slow-spreading pool of blood, and a champagne-pink feather floating on the surface.

Down below me, I hear a door open and then close. I want to flee, to run, but there's nowhere to go. Mother wouldn't go with me, even if there were. I can't leave her behind, so I go back into our rooms and wait. Through the crack beneath the door, I see the lights in the hallway gutter and go out. I stand between Mother and the door, while the snow continues to fall steadily against the window.

There is an image that torments me as I wait. A moment in Murnau's *Faust*, when Emil Jannings as the Devil stands above the city, his black wings spread as wide as the sky. As I hear footsteps on the stairs, I look out our window at the feathered clouds, the downy snow that keeps falling forever without cease, and I wonder what fell spirit holds us in his wings.

AUTHOR'S NOTES:

I wrote this one as a companion piece to "The White Prince," this time exploring vampire imagery from early silent horror films, which was often very different from the red satin cape and widow's peak that became the standard after Bela Lugosi's iconic turn as Dracula in 1931. It was for the special "wings"-themed fourteenth issue of *Innsmouth Magazine*, which is why there are so many references to birds and feathers, and it was later produced as an audio podcast for *Pseudopod*. (The third story I sold to them, after "The Worm That Gnaws" earlier in this book and "Black Hill" in my previous collection.)

I may have fudged a bit on chronology in this one, since I'm not actually sure when all of the great German silent films that I refer to in the story got wide release here in the States, but I *really* wanted them in here, especially that image of Emil Jannings as the Devil, which was literally the first note I wrote down when I started working on the story.

THE MURDERS ON
MORGUE STREET

I
t's the middle of the hottest summer on record when they find
the body, though there's not really enough of it left to qualify
as such. No bones, nor much in the way of blood. Just a rubbery skin and no apparent way to have extracted the insides.

They find it in an apartment up off Seventh, a smallish place,
with a metal fan sitting on top of the icebox and faded blue lilies
on the wallpaper. The smell of it fills the room up, the dark, damp
cellar smell of fresh corpses, and something else, underneath, like
wet fur.

It was the smell that triggered the phone call that led the officers here. The woman that once wore the body was a mother,
but her ten-year-old daughter is staying with family for the summer. Somewhere out in the country, somewhere cooler. The officers who knocked on the door are still standing nearby, one out
in the hallway, one in the kitchen with his head hanging out the
open window, but this is homicide's show. Detective Laughton,
who most of the beat cops know for his mustache and the smell
of his aftershave, and you with him, a criminology student from a
cop family. The word is that your uncle is top brass in another pre-
cinct, that he got you a ride-along with Laughton for the summer.

You stare at the body, not looking away like the officers do.

Detective Laughton squats beside it, shaking his head from side to side. "What the hell?" he keeps asking, over and over again, as though somebody will suddenly have the answer. "What the hell?"

***

Eventually, they load the body into the wagon. Not on a gurney, though; folded up in a crate, like a blanket.

The morgue is in the basement of the county medical examiner's office. Bodies are brought in through the back door, by way of a brick-paved alley known locally as Morgue Street. That's where Detective Laughton parks when the call comes in telling him that the body has disappeared. Night has fallen by the time you arrive, but the coming of darkness does nothing to relieve the heat.

"I think it's going to rain," Detective Laughton says as he gets out of the car. You look up, at the stars that are like smudges against the night. There isn't a cloud in the sky.

Inside, the morgue is full of activity. Officers in uniform pace everywhere, taking statements, talking to everyone. The coroner is a short man with a bulging belly who always talks like he has a head cold. He assures Detective Laughton, "just as I told the other officers," that the body was never delivered, even though a quick check of the logbooks shows the driver's arrival and the delivery of one body, thereafter unaccounted for.

"Whose initials are these?" Detective Laughton asks, pointing to a dark scribble next to the delivery, but the coroner just shakes his head.

The driver, a man about your age, is sitting in a side room with bare walls, his head held in his hands. He looks like he's about to cry. "I gave it to Carl," he says, Carl being one of the coroner's assistants, who has already sworn that he hasn't received a delivery all day. "We've known each other for years. Why would he say I didn't? Why would he lie?"

"What's going to happen to him?" you ask, as you walk back to the car.

Detective Laughton shakes his head. "Not our problem," he says. "They're probably in on it," with a jerk of his head back to include the coroner, his assistant, and the driver all in one vague motion. "Go home. We'll worry about it in the morning. It's not like she's going to get any deader."

***

Home is a fifth-floor apartment that looks out over train tracks and a couple of rooftops, but that's not where you go. Detective Laughton drops you off and you walk down to a little basement theatre called the Orpheus, one of many such theatres to bear the name. You're seeing a girl named Deidre who sells tickets there, and most nights you find your way down to the theatre and either flirt with her, if she's not too busy, or else buy a ticket to the show if she is.

There's a new act that started just this week. "The Amazing Dr. Mirakle," a mesmerist. You remember Deidre mentioning it when you round the corner and see the marquee. "He can make a person do just about anything," she said. "Cluck like a chicken, turn a cartwheel, and they don't remember a thing about it afterward."

When you walk up Deidre looks beautiful, but busy, harried, one strand of her blonde hair come loose and dangling in front of her face, where she keeps blowing it aside as she counts out money and tears off tickets. "I'll take one," you say, walking up to the booth.

"The show's already started," she cautions, smiling.

"That's all right. This way I'll be here when you get off." She looks grateful, tears off a ticket and hands it to you.

You push through the curtained doorway and into the audi-torium. It's smoky, dim. The stage is small, the setting intimate. More like a big parlor than a theatre. You find a seat near the back, looking down across the backs of people's heads to the stage where a striking figure stands before the audience. He wears a coat-and-tails, holds a brass-topped cane in his hand. A top hat sits on a stool behind him as he bows and speaks to the audience, obviously having just completed some feat.

Dr. Mirakle's face is white, his eyes dark and sunken. His hair grows into a natural widow's peak, and is swept away from his face to curl slightly at the back. He speaks with a faint Eastern European accent that he disguises well enough to make it almost impossible to place.

"No doubt you have seen other so-called 'hypnotists' perform their chicanery on stage," he says. "But I assure you that my work is different. I have studied under some of the great minds of Europe, perfecting Herr Mesmer's theories of animal magnetism. You see no dangling pendulums or spinning boards here, no, but only science!"

He does a trick or two, and he isn't lying about the paraphernalia. There's not a pocket watch or a multi-hued lantern to be found. He simply locks eyes with his volunteer, speaks to them softly, evenly, too quietly to be heard in the audience, then he passes his hands in front of their eyes, down their chests, along their arms, his fingertips barely brushing the fabric of their clothes, and the next thing you know they're performing according to his commands, answering questions in monotone voices that make their wives or husbands, brothers or sisters gasp.

To close his act, he calls a man up onto the stage. He looks somber as he makes the passes with his hands. "Herr Mesmer's work has been relegated to the trade of hypnotists and showmen," he says, as though talking to himself, but loudly enough that the audience can hear. "But he was more than a hypnotist, yes? He was a scientist. He saw in men the animal essence, and he sought to affect it, to control it. But who can say that he fully understands man?"

He steps away from his volunteer, a big, broad-shouldered man with sandy hair and beard. "Now you," he says, obviously speaking to the volunteer now. "What are you?"

In answer, the man drops to all fours, standing on his feet with the palms of his hands on the stage. He swings his head back and forth, snuffling at the air in a manner you've seen before, at the zoo downtown.

"Ah," Dr. Mirakle says, "this man, he has some Norse ancestry, perhaps, yes? The Norse, they believe that by wearing an animal's skin, they can channel that animal's spirit. They wear the bear's skin to become fierce like a bear. *Barsark*, yes? But this man here, he wears no skin, but he is *barsark* all the same, is he not?"

At this the man rises back to his full height, his arms extended out and up, and roars out across the auditorium, a terrible, animal sound that no human throat should ever make.

Deidre said that he could make people quack like a duck, but this isn't a man being made to roar like a bear. From where you sit you can see the man's eyes, see the way they gleam when the light strikes them. This man is lost completely. For all intents and purposes, it is a bear who stands up on the stage before you.

Then Dr. Mirakle snaps his fingers and the illusion—if it was an illusion—is dispersed. The man is just a man again, and slowly, sheepishly he folds his arms back to his sides, his eyes already searching in the crowd for the woman he was sitting beside, the question visible in his gaze, "What did I do?"

After the show, as the other audience members file out, you think to approach Dr. Mirakle, to ask him a question. He hasn't retreated backstage like most showmen, but is walking to and fro, picking up items with the help of a big thuggish assistant who looks like he'd be more at home on the docks than on a stage, even a shabby one like the Orpheus.

You introduce yourself, and Dr. Mirakle smiles, bows slightly, shakes your hand. "A pleasure," he says. "And what can I do for you?"

You make yourself meet his gaze, to see if you feel anything unusual. His eyes are dark, surprisingly deeply-set, but up close you can see that they're just brown. You feel no shiver, no clouding of your mind.

"I had a question," you say. "Could a person be..." You stop, searching for the word.

"Hypnotized is fine," Dr. Mirakle says. "It is a name used by parlor tricksters, but in reality, it is as good as any."

"Hypnotized, then," you say with a nod, "so that they didn't remember what they had done, to whom they had spoken, or given an item? Or so that they remembered it falsely?"

"Certainly," he says. "I believe that the untapped potential of the human mind is greater than anyone imagines, and that if the mind can be brought into agreement with itself, almost anything can be achieved using only its power."

"How could someone find out what had happened during such a period?" you ask.

Dr. Mirakle shakes his head. "Without finding the one who hypnotized them? It would be impossible."

***

Detective Laughton turns out to be right, and the next day the heat wave finally breaks and a storm rolls in with driving rain. It's your day off from the ride-along, and so you sit in your apartment in your old armchair. It's pleasantly cool, like the underside of a pillow that you flip over in the middle of the night, and there's a kettle of water on the stove for tea.

You're dozing in your chair when the lock on your door rattles. It takes you a moment to rouse yourself, and by then the first blow has already fallen against the door. It's followed by another, and then the door is crashing open, leaning drunkenly on hinges half-pulled from the wall. In the doorway stands something that you think, for one bleary-eyed second, might be a big man, but no, it's something else. A beast, its limbs long, its face brutish and square, with thick brows and jutting yellow teeth. Tucked under one of its arms is a folded, rubbery parcel, like a raincoat, that drips water onto the floor as the ape advances on you.

It covers the ground fast, and you're still drowsy, but fortunately the shock galvanizes you and you throw yourself aside as its paw tears the stuffing from your chair. Your first thought is, of course, the door, which still hangs half-open, but the ape is between you and your exit, and its limbs are long and powerful, so you lunge for the kitchenette instead.

The kettle of water is still on the stove, steam now whistling from its spout. You grab the handle and dash its contents into the ape's face. It roars and stumbles backward, clawing at its eyes, dropping the rubbery parcel which you can just see beginning to unfold.

That's when you run.

***

You call Detective Laughton from a payphone. He meets you outside your building—you wait for him under the grocer's awning across the street—and you go in together. The rain is still coming down, and your hair is soaked and dripping, you shirt clinging to your shoulders.

Detective Laughton has his gun out as you climb the stairs, which reassures you. Not because you think the ape will still be there, not by now, but because it means he's taking you seriously, not just humoring you.

The door to your apartment hangs open, and beyond it your room has been torn apart. Not ransacked, as a thief might, but absolutely destroyed, as if by an enraged animal.

The mattress and springs have been hurled from the bed and lie on the floor, wire coils poking out like broken bones. Your chair is snapped in two, your table overturned and split down the middle. One of your kitchen drawers has been hurled at the wall, leaving behind a trail of cutlery.

The ape, however, is long gone, and you're not surprised when Detective Laughton questions your neighbors and finds that nobody saw it come or go.

***

You go to stay with Deidre while Detective Laughton attempts to fill out reports, and while you're there you begin to formulate your theories. You're still thinking, your mind absent, when Deidre leaves, kissing you on the cheek on her way out the door to work. It's not until after she's gone that you recall your night in the theatre, the performance you saw there, and the connections come crashing into place. You rush, hatless, out into the night, hailing a taxi to take you to the theatre, but when you get there the lights are already dim. You see a man in a bowtie who you recognize as the owner closing down the ticket booth. "Deidre didn't show up tonight," he says, when you ask him about her, breathless. "And neither did our main attraction. I had to refund tickets, which I haven't done in fifteen years!"

But you're no longer listening. You run down the street, and at another payphone you call Detective Laughton. You tell him to find out where Dr. Mirakle lives, and to pick you up on the way.

***

Though the address of Dr. Mirakle's basement apartment is 212 1/2 Twelfth, the steps that lead down to it are actually in the brick paved alleyway called Morgue Street, not four blocks from the medical examiner's office.

Dr. Mirakle's real name, as Detective Laughton informs you when he pulls up, is Edward Mirkoval, and he isn't really a doctor. Detective Laughton also tells you to stay behind him as he knocks on the door.

You recognize the man who opens it as Dr. Mirakle's assistant from the show, but you're taken off guard by the recognition you see in his face. One of his eyes is filmed over, milky white and obviously useless—a detail you don't remember from the theatre—but the other stares past Detective Laughton and straight at you with a look of such immediate hatred that you stumble back, as if from a palpable blow.

"Erik," a familiar voice calls from inside, "who is it? Show them in."

Grudgingly, the man who must be Erik steps aside. Detective Laughton steps in past him, and you follow, though for a moment you keep your gaze on Erik's, as he seems to barely be able to restrain his desire to attack you.

The one-room apartment looks like it was once a restaurant or a small pub. There are bunk beds like on a sailing ship, a kitchenette, and a heavy wooden table with two chairs. There's also nothing to support any of your suspicions, except for a heavy trapdoor in the back corner.

Dr. Mirakle stands in the kitchenette, his white shirtsleeves rolled up past his elbows, drying his hands on a kitchen towel. "Ah, my young friend from the theatre," he says, smiling. If he has something to hide, he's doing a good job of hiding it. "The one who wished to know about hypnotism, yes? Is there something more I can do for you?"

"I hope so," you reply. "May I introduce Detective Laughton?"

Dr. Mirakle steps forward, reaching out to clasp the detective's hand, the warm smile never faltering from his lips. "Detective," he says, as though trying the word out.

Detective Laughton meets the other man's gaze and gives his hand a firm shake. "A pleasure," he says reflexively, taken off guard by the warm greeting.

"Indeed," Dr. Mirakle replies, not releasing his hand. "Would you like anything to drink, Detective?"

"No."

"Is your friend here armed, Detective?"

"No."

"Good, then please, give me your gun."

You curse yourself, as you feel the vise-like grip of Erik's arms wrapping around you, pinning your own arms to your sides, forcing you to watch helplessly as Detective Laughton silently, unblinkingly pulls his gun from its holster and hands it to Dr. Mirakle, who in turn trains the barrel on you.

"Why not just hypnotize me too?" you ask.

"I tried," Dr. Mirakle says, his voice regretful. "Some people, they prove resistant. So other measures become necessary."

"Where's Deidre?" you ask, teeth clenched.

"She's safe," Dr. Mirakle says, pacing in front of you, his eyes downcast, his face thoughtful, "but I can see you still don't comprehend. You think me a killer, perhaps?"

"And aren't you?"

He shakes his head, almost sadly, as though he's disappointed in you. "To be a killer I must first have killed, and I have harmed no one. Indeed, everything that I have done has been for the good of others. But it will be easier for you, I think, if I show you. Detective, if you would get the door for us?"

Silently, Detective Laughton obeys, walking robotically across the room and hauling up the trapdoor. Erik lifts you as if you weigh nothing and carries you over to the dank steps that lead down into the sub-basement of the building.

The room below is enormous, with great stone arches that, you imagine, must once have held barrels of liquor. Now they hold cages with thick iron bars, like the ones used in the circus, all but one of them occupied by pacing beasts; a wolf, a bear, and a sleek black panther.

You scan the room, looking for Deidre. You've seen the serial pictures, you expect to find her chained up to an operating table, or drugged on some altar. Instead, you see a series of wooden racks hung with human skins, their limbs splayed out as if left there to dry. And on the farthest end, identifiable only by the blue dress that still hangs loosely on it, the blonde hair that now dangles like a discarded wig, you recognize Deidre.

You shriek, spit, strain as hard as you can against Erik's iron grip. "Please," Dr. Mirakle says, as your struggles finally cease, as you hang there spent and sweating. "Do not resist further. I would hate to have to shoot you before you can be made to understand. You believe the girl you love is dead now, yes? But I tell you she is not. She is free, freer than she has ever been."

"Liar," you shout, struggling again, kicking your feet against Erik's shins until he squeezes tighter, until you see lights bursting in front of your vision, and finally darkness claims you.

***

You wake manacled, one wrist encased in a metal clasp, a length of chain connecting you to the wall. Instantly you test it, and Dr. Mirakle stands imperturbably by until you have quieted. "Now," he says, "if you are quite finished, I will explain to you, in a way that even you must comprehend. Erik, please, a demonstration?"

Erik steps forward, directly in front of you, and involuntarily you flinch back. But he doesn't advance. Instead, his head tips back and his mouth yawns open, inhumanly wide, the skin around his lips stretching and splitting. And then a dark head pokes out, followed by thick, hairy hands and then a hulking, shaggy body. When it has stepped completely free from its cast-off skin, you recognize the ape from your apartment, its face scarred with burns, one eye milky and useless.

You feel your mind become suddenly slippery. The sight of Deidre's skin hung there on the rack was only prelude to this, now, as you realize that all your suppositions were insufficient. You had connected Dr. Mirakle to the ape, yes, to the murders, to the theft of the body, to the mysterious gaps in everyone's memory. You had imagined him hypnotizing the men to forget, the ape to do his bidding. You had guessed that, by questioning him, you strayed too near the truth. But you had not imagined, *could not* have imagined, this.

"Erik was my first success," Dr. Mirakle is saying. "He has been with me since the beginning. The others are more recent successes."

"Successes?" The word seems to catch in your throat, barely manages to leave your mouth as you struggle, feeling the very edges of what it must be like to just give up, to go mad.

"Man is an impure, contradictory creature," Dr. Mirakle replies. "The 'highest animal,' yes? But he tries at all turns to suppress his animal side, and instead he turns to drugs, to drink. Animals do not suffer from angst. They are not vengeful, spiteful, cruel. Only men are. Only men kill each other to no purpose, and drug themselves to dull the pain of living. And yet, within each man lives a beast, an animal essence, pure and unencumbered by man's miseries and yearnings. You believe I have killed these people, but I have set them free!"

As he speaks, you're struggling with your bonds, working your wrist back and forth almost mechanically, your mind desperately scrabbling to process what you now know. Is it possible? Is one of the animals in those cages really Deidre? Your eyes slide across them, and your gaze catches the glance of the panther, and do you see, in those yellow eyes, some vestige, some spark of the woman you think you might have loved?

You have no plan, as you pull your hand free of the manacle. No idea what you'll do with your liberty, with the next few seconds, with the rest of your life. Just as your hand slips its bond, you hear Detective Laughton's tread on the stairs, his trance apparently broken during Dr. Mirakle's soliloquy.

Surprised, Dr. Mirakle turns and fires before he has even seen. The bullet strikes Detective Laughton in the stomach, and you hear him make a sound like a bleating sheep. Without thinking, without time to think, you rush toward him and Dr. Mirakle, seeing your movement, turns to fire on you. But Erik is faster, is already moving to intercept you, and Dr. Mirakle's bullet strikes him instead. He stumbles and collapses at your feet with a whimpering, deflating sound.

Dr. Mirakle stares, at Erik and then at the gun in his hand. "What have you done?" he asks. You're already running as the gun raises again to follow you, already going to do the only thing you can think of *to* do as you throw the lever that opens the big iron cages.

The gun roars again, and you feel a blast of heat in your leg and you fall, but your work is already done.

Dr. Mirakle is right, animals aren't vengeful. But the animals in the cages lack Erik's loyalty to their maker, and as soon as their prisons are open they all rush for the stairs. Dr. Mirakle is terrified now, mad, and he fires wildly at them as they charge. The bear, ignoring his desperate shots, brushes him aside with a blow that lays him open and smashes him against the basement wall like a broken toy.

Erik, wounded but not yet dead, throws himself in the way of his master's killers. He catches the front legs of the wolf as it pounces, and they go down together in a frenzy of blood and fur, but the fight cannot last. Erik is wounded, and in seconds the wolf raises its bloody muzzle and follows the others to the stairs. Only the panther stops at the foot and turns back, looks once at you where you lie on the floor. Then she too, is gone.

***

The rest becomes a blur. Dimly, you remember crawling to Detective Laughton's side and finding him alive but unconscious. You remember the police arriving, though you don't remember what you tell them. It doesn't really matter. As far as they're concerned, Dr. Mirakle's collection of human skins and his now-absent menagerie are simply two different halves of his clearly fractured psyche, the unrelated eccentricities of a lunatic.

Detective Laughton must suspect that something more than murder went on there that night, but he never asks you about it. You give up criminology, and though your family is obviously disappointed and confused, Detective Laughton rests his hand on your shoulder and nods, as though he understands.

Throughout it all, and for the rest of your days, it's the backward glance of those yellow eyes that haunts you. You keep in touch with Deidre's family, and they move on, and they never see her again, and you never tell them what you know, or think you know. You think about it every day, though you try to forget. It's there in every crowd, in every handshake. Even when you're an old man, retired and with a bad heart, you still can't help but wonder, when you look at yourself in the mirror every night, what sort of beast is staring back at you, waiting.

AUTHOR'S NOTES:

Okay, hands up if you remember those old Crestwood House Monster books; the first series had orange covers, the second series had purple, both were retellings of classic monster films, complete with lots and lots of black-and-white photos. When I was a kid my school library had most of them, and I read them compulsively.

I think a lot of the way my imagination works was formed by paging through those old books and others like them, staring hard at the stills from movies that I had never seen, and imagining what they must have been like. Years later I would see most of those movies, and many of them would be wonderful in their own right, but they were never quite like the movies that screened in my mind when I pored over those images.

"The Murders on Morgue Street" is *kind of* inspired by

Poe's original story, and *kind of* by Clive Barker's retelling from *The Books of Blood*, but mostly it's inspired by the wonderful 1932 adaptation starring Bela Lugosi. Or, more accurately, it's inspired by the Crestwood House book about the movie, from which I lifted the names of Dr. Mirakle and his ape, Erik. Detective Laughton is named—I think unconsciously, at the time—for the great Charles Laughton, who I first encountered in *The Old Dark House*, probably my favorite horror flick of the '30s. Laughton was also in *Island of Lost Souls*, which left an imprint on this story as well, along with some of the great Val Lewton films of the period.

I originally wrote this—in a very different form—for a Poe-themed anthology many years ago. It didn't make it in, but I liked the idea, so I kept tinkering with it and rewriting it now and again over the years until it ended up in the shape you see here. This is its first time in print.

RIPPEROLOGY

"It is a blessed condition, believe me.
To be whispered about at street corners.
To live in other people's dreams, but not to have to be."
                              —*Candyman* (1992)

I t was my grandfather who taught me the difference between a man and a monster. I remember him saying, "When a man dies, that's the end of his power. A monster is different. When a monster dies, its power is just beginning." We were watching Bela Lugosi as Dracula at the time, on the big old black-and-white, wood-panel TV that sat in my grandfather's living room until the day he died.

He died in his sleep. Nothing terribly dramatic. They said that his heart just stopped. Though he had always seemed old to me, he never seemed weak or sick. In his last years, he often sat very still, staring off at nothing, or at something only he could see. He seemed like a golem, like a figure carved roughly from stone, hard and unyielding.

My grandfather was Jewish, by birth but not by practice. He had survived the Holocaust, had a number tattooed on his wrist and everything, just like in a movie. My mother said that he had been religious when he was a boy, but that the Holocaust had knocked his faith right out of him. I asked him once if he still believed, and he told me, "I believe in the God of Abraham, and that God is a motherfucker."

My mother and I lived in his house when I was growing up, until he died. When I broke one of his rules, he would whip me with his belt. I can remember the sound that belt made when he took it off; a clear, purposeful sound. I was afraid of him, but I was also enthralled by him. When he told me something, I listened as I never listened to anyone else, before or since.

When he died, my fear and my fascination died with him. I guess he was just a man, after all.

***

Why do we have a name for the study of Jack the Ripper? Why are men fascinated by him after all these years? Why the books, the movies, all of it? Jack the Ripper killed five people. Just five. And that's assuming that all were killed by the same hand. Others have killed more, in much more spectacular fashion, before and since. Sawney Bean and his clan, eating people in the Scottish hills of the 15th Century. Just five years after the Ripper murders, H. H. Holmes killed as many as two hundred people in ways a thousand times more fanciful and grotesque than anything the Ripper was ever accused of, but hardly anyone knows his name today. What's the difference?

It's really quite simple. With Holmes we have a name, a face, a photograph. We feel that we know him. We can say, "He did these black deeds, but he was still only a man." The power of the Ripper comes from the fact that he isn't a man. The hand that held the blade may have belonged to a man, or a woman, or to several people. That isn't important. It doesn't matter if the name was Sir William Gull, Lewis Carroll, or Mary Pearcey. That is why the legend of the Ripper is immune to every explanation, every suspect. No theory will ever satisfy, because the Ripper was much more than the hand that held the knife. Something that probably didn't yet exist at all when the first throat was cut. Something that may not have existed yet even when the last woman was dead. Its first faint stirrings could be felt when the killer was given a name. The heartbeat quickened as letters began to pour into police stations and newspapers, claiming to be from the Ripper. Suddenly, the Ripper was no longer just a killer, but had become something that was alive in every heart, sending letters out not by human agency, but from Hell itself.

No theory, no proof, will ever quench men's thirst for the Ripper legend, because the Ripper can never be contained by any one suspect, or conspiracy, or narrative. In Madame Tussauds' Chamber of Horrors he is represented only by a shadow, the last and final word on the Ripper's legacy.

—from *Every Man Jack*, by Derek Midwinter

***

Derek's table was next to mine at the Ghosts and Gangsters Convention in Chicago. During one of the many lulls between people walking by and listlessly fingering our books before moving off without buying a copy or asking for an autograph, he leaned over and introduced himself. "I need a beverage if I'm going to make it through this," he said. "You watch my table, and I'll bring you back something?"

He wore a three-piece suit, even though most of the other people aimlessly making the rounds were dressed in black t-shirts and jeans. His hair was long and white, with a beard to match, though he seemed to only be in his energetic fifties. When I shook his hand, I noticed that it felt strangely dry and smooth, like worn leather, like he was wearing an expensive glove. When I notice things like that, I try to imagine myself writing them down in a notebook in my head, so that I'll remember them later, when I'm back in front of my computer. I picture the words appearing in the notebook, written down by a phantom pen, *like an expensive glove.* It's my process; it works for me.

When Derek came back from the bar with a glass of beer in each hand, we got to talking, and that's when we learned that we both lived in Kansas City. If you spend any time at all in any kind of niche hobby, you quickly figure out that it's a small world. Anyone who does anything in it gets to know almost everyone else, and that goes double if you live in the Midwest, rather than New York or LA or someplace. It may not have been a lot, but it was enough to get us talking that night at the convention, and that was enough to get things started.

Derek stood out. He was what you'd call gregarious, though it also didn't take him long to put people off. He spoke like a lecturer, and I wasn't surprised to learn that he'd been an attorney before going on disability due to an undisclosed condition. He walked with a slight limp, but rumor had it that it was a psychological malady that kept him from practicing, rather than a physical one. Whichever it was, Derek never shared the nature of it with me.

He'd written two books on Jack the Ripper, one on Ed Gein, one on H. H. Holmes. All of them nonfiction, none of them really about the murders themselves. Instead he concerned himself with the cultural repercussions of the crimes, the narratives that had been built up around them. The ties between Ed Gein and *Psycho*, *The Texas Chainsaw Massacre*, and our modern idea of the serial killer, that kind of thing. "People like to compare actors and superheroes to the gods and demigods of Greek myth," he said in a lecture at that same convention, "but really it's the murderers who form the backbone of our cultural mythology. What does that say about us?"

He was at the convention peddling his second Ripper book, and from talking to him I quickly learned that, while he had come to Ripperology rather late in his career as a ghoul (his word), it had rapidly become the focus of his mania. He'd gotten his start in the field as a collector of murder memorabilia. The old-fashioned wire glasses that hid his dark eyes were actually part of his collection, worn by a clerk who worked the Holmes case in 1893, painstakingly restored and fitted with Derek's prescription. "No reason to assume that they saw anything to do with it, of course," he told me once, leaning conspiratorially over his beer, "but then again, no reason to assume they *didn't*, either."

***

The first time I went to Derek's big house on Holmes Street—not an accident, he told me—it was to see his collection. I was writing my third and longest book for Cold Blood Press, purveyors of local-interest true crime fiction, about the Bloody Benders. When Derek learned that, he told me that he had, in his collection, several pieces from the old Bender Museum in Cherryvale, from when it got shut down and turned into a fire station.

Derek was a bachelor, with a grown daughter from a marriage that had ended fifteen years before I met him. His house was nice, clean and meticulous, filled with books and real wood furniture. He had a wine cabinet, though I only ever saw him drink wine on two occasions.

He kept his collection in the basement. It wasn't at all dim or disordered, like it would have been in a police procedural or a scary movie. Derek was a collector, not a hoarder, and his collection was as meticulously organized as a museum vault. Carefully preserved, coded and catalogued, grouped together by murder and ordered by year. Nothing very new, aside from a few Ed Gein pieces left over from when he was researching his first book. Mostly, he was fascinated with murders from around the turn of the century. But there weren't any Jack the Ripper pieces in his collection.

When I asked him about it, he just shrugged, but then he brought it up again, out of the blue, later that night. "I don't really know why," he said, suddenly, in the midst of a lull in conversation. "My mania for collecting just seems to have petered out about the same time my mania for the Ripper really came on. Not that Ripper memorabilia is exactly easy to come by, anyway."

He may not have known why, but privately I think that it was just the evolution of his obsession. While he may have started out as a collector, it was always the way that we mythologize killers that really interested him. His collection was just an entry point to understand that process, beginning with fetishizing the accoutrements of the crimes, and moving from there to the metaphysics of the crimes themselves. Though Ripperology was never my thing, I'd read a few books on it before, and I read both of Derek's, and Derek was the only Ripperologist I ever knew of who didn't have a theory as to Jack's identity. In fact, Derek seemed to think that there was more to the Ripper mythos than any one identity could ever contain. That was essentially the thesis of his second Ripper book, *Every Man Jack*.

After Derek's death, the police asked me if I was his friend, and I wasn't sure how to answer. I guess that I was probably the best friend he had. We were both bachelors, both writers, both in the same field. We lived twenty minutes away from one another, in good traffic. I went to his house a few times, he came to mine more seldom. We used to meet for drinks at a bar on the Plaza called Sullivan's. I knew him for six years, but I never met his daughter, he never even told me the name of the firm where he used to work. When we got together it was our interests we talked about, not our lives. For the first two years, I assumed that Midwinter wasn't even his real last name, just something he put on because it looked better on the cover than Jones or Meyers, until I happened to see a utility bill on his kitchen table addressed to it.

***

Unlike my grandfather, Derek didn't die quietly in his sleep. And unlike my grandfather, I wasn't the one who found his body. He had a lady who came in twice a week to dust and vacuum and do the laundry, and she found him sitting in a chair in his basement, surrounded by his collection, a cutthroat razor in his lap and both of his hands nearly hacked off. The wrists not just slit, but sawed through, cut all the way around to the bone, as though he was trying to remove his hands like gloves. The coroner said that the tendons were severed in both hands. They had no idea how he'd managed to hold the razor at the end. The working theory was that he gripped it in his teeth.

He left behind no note, no indication of why he had done it. The police conducted an investigation, but there was no sign of forced entry or burglary, and they had no leads. Derek kept a careful catalog of his collection, and every item in it was accounted for. All signs pointed to a bizarre and inexplicable suicide, case closed. It's what everyone assumed, his daughter included, and in their assumptions you could hear, unvoiced, the old refrains about his undisclosed mental condition, about the morbidity of his hobbies. I was asked only cursory questions during the investigation, and I didn't have anything to add that would shed any light.

I went to Derek's house for the last time when the estate sale was happening. His daughter lived in Seattle, and while she flew down for the funeral, she had everything sold through an agency. Derek's collection went up on an online auction site and brought quite a bit of money. I didn't buy anything from it, though I bought a chair from his house at the regular auction, one that I used to sit in next to the bay window when we would drink and talk about crimes committed before we were born.

They moved most of the furniture out onto the lawn to sell it. Somehow, doing that divorced it from him, made it into just stuff, all disarrayed and random. Like a dissection or an anatomical chart, just shapes now with numbers tacked on, nothing left that resembled a person, resembled a life. People were wandering through it in the fall weather, kicking dead leaves off the lawn and pulling the drawers out of dressers. I was standing on the front walk, looking up at the house, and my glance fell on the cupola window above the front porch, where Derek used to sit and watch the traffic go by when he couldn't sleep. A figure was standing there, just a shadow against the glare of the window, but one that I knew instantly, though I had never seen it before. It was a figure that anyone alive would recognize. Tall and indistinct, in a top hat and cape, his white-gloved hands crossed at his waist.

Maybe I should have gone in then and investigated. Maybe I would have found that it was just some eccentric collector, another enthusiast come to gather memorabilia from Derek's old life. But seeing that figure there, feeling his unseen gaze on me, I felt sick, like the sidewalk was buckling under my feet, and I turned and walked away, sat sweating in my car on the side of the road until I felt well enough to drive home.

***

The day after the estate sale, I got a package in the mail from Derek, postmarked the day that he'd killed himself. I called the post office, and they said he'd left instructions to delay postage. They'd assumed that it was a birthday present or something.

Inside there was no note, no explanation. Nothing to clarify the nightmare jumble of his death. Just one object, carefully wrapped and sealed, something that hadn't been listed on his exhaustive collection manifest. A single white opera glove, with a brownish-red stain around the cuff.

That night, I had a dream. In it, I watched myself sleeping from a vantage point somewhere up near the corner of my ceiling. From there I couldn't see the glove extract itself from its nest of packaging on my kitchen table, but I heard the rustling and I saw it appear like a plump, pale spider in my bedroom doorway. Bodiless as a dreamer, powerless to intervene, I watched it creep across the floor and up my sleeping body. When it fastened itself around my throat I felt its grip, dry and smooth.

That was the last night that I slept. I spend a lot of time now sitting and looking out my own window at the street below, waiting for a familiar shadow to cross my path. In life I was fascinated by Derek Midwinter. In death, he terrifies me. I guess maybe now he's become the monster after all.

AUTHOR'S NOTES:

When Ross Lockhart approached me to contribute a story to *Tales of Jack the Ripper*, I was happy to oblige, though I wasn't sure what I could add to the vast tracts of fiction, nonfiction, and Gull chasing that had already been written on the subject. After circling it a few times myself, and going back to some classics like Alan Moore's *From Hell*, I was finally inspired by the quote from *Candyman* that opens the story, to write a tale speculating on the nature of the lasting appeal of Jack, and why no theory or explanation as to his identity would ever suffice, even if we were to strike upon one with sufficient substance to actually qualify as proof.

The story's ending scenes owe a substantial debt to a great Fritz Leiber tale called "The Glove." This is one of a handful of stories I've written set explicitly in Kansas City, and the little Kansas town of Cherryvale, where the Bender Museum once stood, is a real place where I've spent the night a few times, though sadly the museum was already gone by the time I went there.

WALPURGISNACHT

O n the train, Nicky told me about the Brocken Spectre. "It's a sort of optical illusion," he said, leaning forward, his elbows on his knees. Nicky was younger than me, and prettier, and his dark hair fell in front of his face whenever he slouched, which was often. "The sun casts a giant shadow of you on the clouds below, right, and your head gets this prismatic halo. Like an angel."

"I hear the sun only shines here like sixty days a year," I said. "Besides, it's night." I was only half-listening anyway, my head lolling against the cool glass of the window. I'd had more than a few drinks at the airport bar, and I could feel a headache trying to force its way out past my eyes. Outside, I could see our destination looming up out of the darkness, the two towers of the *Sender Brocken*, old and new. Like Tolkien's Minas Morgul and Orthanc. The sun was still going down, and the towers stood out like shadows against the gloaming, their lights already on. Gleaming yellow ones in the windows of the old tower, now the Brocken Hotel, and blinking red ones to warn planes away from the new tower, a candy cane-striped lance that jutted skyward from the peak.

"It doesn't look terribly inviting," Nicky said, noticing my inattentiveness and nodding at the towers.

"Now to the Brocken the witches ride," I intoned, and then, without bothering to glance and see his puzzled expression, explained,

"It's Goethe. From *Faust*."

That was why we were going, of course. It was Walpurgisnacht, the night when the witches and devils gathered on the crown of the bald mountain to welcome the spring. Nicky and I, and whoever else was on the train with us, were the witches in this equation, and we were all gathering on the Brocken to kiss the ass of a black goat.

***

We met Henri at the Steadman Gallery. Nicky had some of his photographs there, as part of a show called "The New Decadence." From his "Conqueror Worm" cycle—my name—all graveyards and ossuaries, done in lots of blues and greens with the occasional splash of red or yellow. A leaf, a salamander. They were good pictures, some of Nicky's best, in my opinion, and I guess Henri thought so, too.

I don't remember the other stuff in the show, but I remember Henri. Tall, old-fashioned handsome, Van Dyke beard, clothes like a Vincent Price villain. He carried a cane that was pure affectation, black wood with an amethyst top. He was a regular in the galleries, though word was that he spent more time in Europe than the States. Why he was in New York that year, I never learned, just as I never learned his real name. DuPlante was the most common surname associated with him, but how accurate it was, I can't say. Henri kept as much about himself veiled in mystery as he could, kept himself interesting.

Even before we'd met, I'd heard about him. Rich, listless, a Decadent of the old school. He was known for throwing wild parties with strange themes, and for occasionally throwing large wads of money at young artists who caught his fancy, which meant that Nicky and I were of course very happy to make his acquaintance, to catch his eye.

Where exactly all his money came from was the subject of some speculation. One story went that his father was a lord, another that he was heir to a fortune in pornography. Some said that he'd been some kind of *wunderkind* and had invented some patent as a child and still lived off the dividends.

There were lots of stories about Henri, many of them contradictory, but he seemed to welcome all of them. There was only one that I had ever known him to actively refute. Supposedly he had an older sister, one whose tastes made Henri's seem positively Puritan by comparison. Some people claimed to have met her, though never in his company. They always described her the same way, which was odd. Tall, dark hair, stylishly dressed. Always named Alexandria. I was so bold as to ask Henri about it once, but he replied, with uncharacteristic clarity, "I'm an only child."

"Maybe she was an old lover," Nicky hypothesized once. "Somebody who just pretended to be his sister." It was certainly kinky enough.

Real or imagined, Henri didn't like to talk about her. The subject made him visibly uncomfortable, was maybe the only subject I'd ever come across that did.

Luckily for him, I was less concerned with stories about where Henri's money came from, and more concerned with where it went. The fact was, he spent it like water and never wanted for more, and Nicky and I had expensive tastes and no inclination to a hard day's work, so men like Henri were bread and butter for us.

At the Steadman Gallery, he kissed Nicky's hand but shook mine. He struck me then as I would continue to think of him throughout our acquaintance: as a spoiled dandy who enjoyed playing the beast because it amused him, more than because there was much actual beast in him.

Aside from his money and his interest in the arts, he was known mostly for what he called his "revels." "Party," he said to me once, "is far too small a word." I don't remember how many of them Nicky and I attended in the years that we knew Henri. Nicky always brought his camera, and he got a couple of decent series out of them, neither of them half as good as the work he was doing when we met, but then, booze and drugs and other temptations flowed freely at the revels, and Nicky was no less susceptible to them than I, and they took their toll on both of us, in different ways.

How to describe one of Henri's revels? He once told a reporter, "I take intent, and marry it with time and place." Which isn't really very helpful, either. I guess that fundamentally they *were* just parties, on a grand scale, complete with the kinds of party games that would have shocked and titillated Victorians, but Henri saw them—or maybe he just *sold* them—as something more like performance art. A séance held at midnight in a haunted hotel. A black mass in the catacombs under Paris. Diversions for the bored and the rich and the morbid. Nicky and I were two of those, and Henri was rich enough for everybody.

This one, though, the one atop the Brocken, on Walpurgisnacht, was supposed to be different. More intimate, more personal, and his last. That's what the invitations had said. Henri had supposedly discovered a rare film print by Eadweard Muybridge, something suitably infernal, not just studies of animals in motion, and he was going to screen it for a few dozen of his closest friends at midnight, "in its native habitat." There was to be a small chamber orchestra, and Henri had reserved the entire hotel, so we wouldn't be disturbed. "Unless of course some other witches decide to drop in."

***

When the train pulled up to the station, Nicky and I got out, along with a few others that I recognized from Henri's inner circle, and still more that I didn't. Maybe new additions, maybe lapsed recruits pulled back in for one last hurrah. I helped Nicky shoulder one of his camera bags, and we all walked down to the cars that were waiting to take us the rest of the way to the top of the mountain.

We shared our car with a girl who looked young, and too thin for my tastes. She was wearing a black dress, with diamonds glittering at her wrists and neck, and silver hair that was probably a wig but might have been some impressive dye job. Nicky pulled out his camera and held it up, giving her a quizzical look to which he received a nod and giggle. He snapped several photos on the car ride up, flattering her, I'm sure, but I knew that he was just warming up, getting ready for the main event.

Would I have accepted Henri's invitation, if it hadn't been for Nicky? I don't know. We'd not had the best time at the last of his revels that we attended, in some hunting lodge in some godforsaken part of Washington state, and it had left a bad taste in my mouth. I couldn't really remember why, too much booze turning the filmstrip of my memory into a series of disassociated snapshots. Something about sitting in the dark by the fire, after the meat of the party was over, playing some idiotic child's game called "Something Scary." I'd never heard of it, but apparently Nicky played it when he was a kid, with his abusive father, the one he never talked about. He told me so afterward, on the car ride home, and he cried and shook in his sleep that night, and didn't say why.

Everything else was blurred, just a bad, sick feeling in the pit of my stomach, but enough that I might have thrown the overwrought bit of paper—with its wax seals and calligraphic script— in the trash, had it not been for the mention of Muybridge. The old photographer fascinated Nicky, and I was happy for anything that got Nicky's attention onto something I found interesting.

The cars deposited us on the foot of the steps leading up to the Brocken Hotel. The building had once been a TV tower, maybe the oldest one in the world, built before World War II. It had transmitted the first live broadcast of the Summer Olympics in Berlin. The war didn't do it any favors, and when the new tower was built they converted the old one into a hotel. The only thing left to mark its former function was the golf ball-like radome that crouched on the roof and held air traffic control equipment.

The lights that had looked so tiny from the train were dazzling up close, but the tower that rose above us, with its tiny windows and the radome on top, reminded me of something from a futuristic prison. Not terribly inviting, as Nicky had said.

Inside, however, the hotel proved to be as luxurious as it had appeared Spartan from without. Red carpets, crystal chandeliers, gilt everything else. We were shown into an enormous ballroom where a projector and screen were set up in pride of place, with couches and divans arrayed for our viewing pleasure. The artwork that normally hung along the walls had been removed, and in its place were easels draped in black cloth. All part of the night's festivities, I assumed.

I knew that Henri himself had dabbled in painting once, when he was younger. I'd never seen the results, but I'd heard that at his best he'd mostly just knocked off Goya. At Henri's one and only gallery opening a critic was apparently overheard to remark, "If you've seen everything Goya ever did, and you still want more, then Henri's the man to talk to," though whether that was intended as condemnation or praise, I couldn't say. By the time Nicky and I met him, he'd already given it up, but his passion for the arts remained a constant throughout his life, so I wasn't exactly surprised to see the easels there.

The man himself was there too, playing the good host and glad-handing his guests as they entered. He looked much as he had the last time I'd seen him, which was also much as he had the *first* time I'd seen him, though now his hair and beard were grayer, and the tiredness that was supposedly driving his retirement could be seen in the corners of his eyes, even as they sparkled as ever with his smile. The years had made him seem distinguished, rather than old, as they were kind enough to do for some people, and he wore his age well.

He kissed Nicky's hand, shook mine, and then he and Nicky were flirting again—Nicky always was flirtatious, Henri always shameless—and then Henri had drifted away to talk to one of the other guests. "It'll be some time before the festivities start," he said over his shoulder as he departed. "The witching hour, and all that. One of the servants can show you to your room, if you'd like to freshen up."

The "servants" were men in coats-and-tails, wearing shapeless *papier-mâché* masks that made them look a bit like disfigured corpses. I knew from previous revels that under the masks I would find invariably young, attractive men, paid well for their forbearance and their discretion.

One of these broke off to escort Nicky and me to our rooms, which were next to each other and connected by an adjoining door. Henri, gracious and accommodating to the last. The rooms were as sumptuously appointed as one might expect, except for the narrow, slit-like windows that were the lasting testament of the building's former function. "There's an observation deck on the roof," the faceless "servant" told me when he saw that I was eyeing the window with some distaste. "It provides a much better view."

I sat down on the bed and kicked off my shoes. The clock on the desk said that I still had almost two hours until midnight, and I was suddenly very tired. The headache from the train was back, and I just wanted to lie down in the dark.

Nicky came from the adjoining room. "I'm going up to the observation deck before the party starts," he said, patting his camera bag. "You want to come?"

I shook my head and lay backward into the softness of the bed. "I think I'm going to take a nap," I said. "Wake me before you go downstairs."

***

He left then, and I slept, or I must have, because I dreamed. In my dream, I had gone with Nicky to the roof. He was standing near the railing, trying to see a Brocken Spectre in the mist that had grown up around the hotel. There was a blindingly white light coming from behind us, maybe from the radome, throwing our shadows out like expressionistic paintings on the rooftop, and across the clouds. I wanted to turn around, to look for the source of the light, but I couldn't. I was staring across the clouds, watching keenly as Nicky tried to position himself to create the halo effect that he was looking for, his camera held up to his face. For some reason, the camera made me uncomfortable. I wanted him to take it down. I had the irrational feeling that he couldn't, that it was welded there. I saw him as some kind of cybernetic Cyclops, staring out through the camera's lens at his own shadow.

I couldn't speak, and there was a distant roaring in my ears, so that I didn't hear Nicky, even as I saw his lips moving. We were not alone on the observation deck. There was a third shadow leaping out across the roof of the clouds, one that didn't seem to shift and move, to jump around as ours did. I tried to turn my head, to see who was standing beside us, but I could only catch a glimpse. It was a woman, straight dark hair, wearing a fur coat, and I knew that it was Alexandria, Henri's older sister, though in the dream she couldn't have been much older than Nicky.

I tried to turn my head, to catch her eye. She was standing behind Nicky, her eyes were dark, holes in a mask that was her face, and her finger was coming up to her lips, shushing me, as though we were sharing a secret. Her shadow and Nicky's shadow were the same, stretching long and dark across the clouds, and he was smiling, the halo appearing around the shadow's head, and the camera snapping and whirring again and again.

***

I sat up in bed. Though the clock said that only a few minutes had passed, a strong wind had come up outside. I could hear it howling against the walls of the building. I turned to look out the window, but the black slit was a mirror against the lights in the room. Still, something was hurtling past through the darkness, something like sparks or embers from a great bonfire, whirled up into the sky in a cyclone.

I got out of bed and walked over to the window, pressing my face against the cold glass and peering out through cupped hands. The night outside was a black maelstrom. The lights of the hotel were gone, and the red warning lights of the opposite tower were lost in the darkness. The only illumination came from the burning shapes that I had originally taken to be sparks but that I saw now were lanterns, lanterns made from human skulls and hollowed gourds. They were carried aloft by figures, some nude, others shrouded in tattered garments whipped by the wind. Some were young, their flesh milky and smooth, while others were impossibly old, their skin puckered, their breasts withered and pendulous. All rode through that swirling darkness, some astride goats and pigs and cats the size of ponies, some on brooms and benches, some carried by owls and vultures and ravens tied on strings.

A woman's voice spoke in my ear, husky and somehow familiar, "*Now to the Brocken the witches ride,*" and then I woke on the bed, still dressed, my face and hands beaded in cold sweat. Again the clock averred that only a few minutes had passed, and I had a moment of lurching terror, the feeling of being trapped in a hallway that you know you have just walked down before. Outside the window the night was merely dark, the wind only a whisper that played along the eaves, the red lights of the *Sender Brocken* blinking their warning.

***

I splashed water on my face, had a drink from the mini bar, and then another. In spite of my earlier instructions to Nicky, I couldn't stay in the room, and I didn't feel like navigating the blind, empty hallways that would take me up to the observation deck, a prospect which left me sick with indefinable horror. Instead I left him a note and went in search of the elevator, which didn't seem like it could possibly be too difficult to locate since I remembered riding it up. Still, I took two wrong turns in the red-and-gold halls trying to find it, and at the second turn I thought I saw someone from the party up ahead, just going around a corner. A flash of silver and fur, a glimpse of a leg, and then she was gone. My first thought was of the girl that had ridden up with us in the car, and I opened my mouth to shout, but then I remembered the woman from my dream, and my voice died in my throat.

By the time I found the elevator and got down to the main floor, it was only twenty minutes to midnight. Buffet tables had been set up in the entryway, covered in brie and strawberries and other delicacies. I passed them by without a second look, because even though I hadn't had a bite since the airport, the very thought of food made my stomach turn.

Inside the ballroom, the black drapes had been removed from the easels. The paintings they revealed must have been Henri's own. They could have passed for Goya in bad light, or at a distance, but their colors were more garish, their subjects more universally grotesque or occult in character. Goya's entire oeuvre, rendered into nothing but Black Paintings. In the largest painting, sitting in a dominant spot along the far wall, warped figures crouched around the form of a massive black goat, an obvious and blatant copy of Goya's *Witches' Sabbath*. More the 1798 one than the 1820s. I walked over to it, and found that there was a title hand-written on a piece of paper and affixed to the easel: "Chernobog."

"Chernobog was a Slavic god, represented by a black he-goat," Henri's voice suddenly said from over my shoulder. "Of course, when the Christians came, he got turned into the devil, like so many others."

"Subtle," I said with a forced smile, turning around and reaching for his hand, not wanting to let him see that he'd startled me.

He smiled himself—his more genuine than mine—and shrugged. "Subtlety, like painting, never really was my strongest suit."

We were momentarily isolated from the noise and bustle of the

room, caught in a bubble of quiet and stillness near the big painting, under the golden eyes of the black goat, and I was still shaken
from my dreams, which seemed to lurch about in my head like
wheeled carts on the deck of a ship. That's probably why I didn't
banter with Henri as I normally might have, and just asked him
straight, "Are you really giving it up? Retiring?"

He nodded, and though his smile didn't falter, his eyes looked
sad. More than just tired, as they had before. Exhausted, spent.
"I'm afraid so," he said. "My time has come. One last revel, and
then it's out, out brief candle."

As he spoke, I saw Nicky come into the gallery out of the corner of my eye, and at the same time Henri looked down at his
wrist, though he didn't wear a watch that I could see. "Speaking of
which, the time is almost upon us. You'll excuse me?"

I nodded and he was gone, lost to the crowd. I started to walk
toward Nicky, but then Henri reappeared, standing near the projector in the center of the room, and everyone was muttering into
silence and Nicky was raising his camera to his eye, and so I froze
where I was.

I can't remember what Henri said, standing there next to the
projector. There was a ringing in my ears, and my headache had
come back full force. I thought I could see someone over his
shoulder, a familiar shape in fur and silver and long, dark hair. No
matter how I moved, though, I couldn't get a clear look.

Henri thanked everyone for coming, and started to talk about
why we were there, about Muybridge and his films. First the stuff
that you could find in the history books—studies of animals in
motion, his murder of his wife's lover and subsequent acquittal—
but no one in the crowd was there for so mundane a scandal,
so then Henri talked about Muybridge's *other* films. Short topics
of occult interest, all of them lost to rumor and speculation and
myth. Some said he'd even caught the Devil Himself on celluloid.

My head was splitting, and I needed to get out of the gallery,
find a drink, hair of the dog. I was pushing past the other revelers,

who all had their gazes fixed forward, on Henri, while my eyes were only for the door. Maybe that's why I saw her there, standing just inside the entrance. Long, dark hair, dark eyes, fur coat. Her hand on the light switch.

The lights went down, and the gallery filled with the whirring sound of the projector. In the flickering silver glow that came from the screen, I could see the faces of the people around me, all of them transformed into pallid, disfigured masks by the play of light and shadow, the "servants" now indistinguishable from the guests. All their eyes were black pits, all staring up at the screen. Reluctantly, I turned to see what they were seeing.

Twenty feet tall, on the wall of the ballroom, three figures wearing conical hats danced in a circle. Their arms were interlocked, their heads down, the points of their hats nearly meeting in the middle as they turned, slowly, rhythmically, like figures on a German clock. Intercut with them were other frames, more animal studies, but wrong this time, donkeys up on their hind legs, turning in a circle. It was just a few frames, figures and donkeys, repeated again and again. Turning and turning, in a dance that would never end.

There was a flicker, then, and the scene changed. A grove, somewhere, in a black forest, dark and thick as the Dore-inspired jungles of Skull Island, but a real place. Fires burned in the background, out of focus, and cloaked figures watched as a young girl, not more than sixteen, coupled with a black goat the size of a bison. Her eyes and mouth were black holes burned in the film. The images moved with the stuttering, shuddering jerkiness of a zoetrope. Just a few frames, turning on an endless loop. A dance that would never end.

The blemish began at the place where the girl met the goat. A rip in the film, a hole that gaped wider and wider as the film burned through, with that familiar sound of bubbling and tearing. For a moment the screen was white, and then there was a crack as glass shattered under extreme heat, and the room was plunged into complete darkness.

It's hard to remember what happened next. The mind almost certainly played tricks at the time, the memory just as surely has played them since. I know that there was a moment of stillness, as the white light burned on the wall of the gallery. I turned in that moment, my eyes searching for the woman I'd seen inside the doorway, but all I saw were our shadows transformed into giants on the walls behind us.

When the light went out completely, there was a sound like a rising tide, as dozens of voices all spoke at once, whether to calm or panic, and dozens of bodies all started to move in different directions. The ringing in my ears seemed to have left my head and spread out into the room itself, and underneath it I would have sworn that I could hear the orchestra playing. Others would later say that they heard it too, some wild, discordant melody that none of us could identify but that we all thought sounded very familiar. Then the whole room tilted, or at least that's how it felt, like the hotel was just a model sitting on a tabletop that somebody had stumbled into.

I felt bodies slamming against me, elbows jamming into my sides, my face. I felt my lip split against bone, I felt myself stumble over someone or something in the dark. Bright strobes of light were going off, and at the time I couldn't account for them, thinking maybe they were going off inside my own head, though now I know that they were the flashbulb of Nicky's camera as he desperately sought to catalogue something of the disaster.

In the flashes, I remember feeling like I had stumbled somehow into one of Henri's paintings. The faces of the people around me seemed bloated and dead, seemed to float up from out of the darkness to assail me. Like I was drowning in a black river, with only corpses to keep me company. The "servants," I told myself later, in their grotesque masks.

I have no clear recollection of making my way outside, but that's where I found myself, my hands on my knees, Nicky trying to staunch the flow of blood from my face. The bright lights of the hotel were on, making our shadows long on the gravel in front of us, turning the night sky into a black dome above our heads. I turned around, and saw that the hotel was on fire. Flames licked out of the doors and windows of the first floor, sending embers spiraling up into the darkness, like lanterns carried aloft.

***

I talked about it later, with the other survivors, with Nicky, with the police. I told them what I had seen, what I could remember, though it didn't seem like much. A few people had been killed in the blaze, many others suffered from burns, smoke inhalation, injuries acquired in the panicked rout. Once the fire was out, they sifted the ruins for bodies, identified the charred remains, sent them back to their families to be buried. Henri wasn't among them. He was never seen again.

When Nicky went to develop his photographs from that night, he told me that none of them came out, from any of the cameras. He said that not even the pictures he'd taken earlier, at the airport and on the train, had returned anything but black squares. He blamed a bad batch of film. He should have been devastated, but he didn't seem to be. After that evening, it was like something turned over inside Nicky. He started photographing again, and turning out good work. The best he'd done in years, but I didn't like them. They reminded me of things I'd seen that night. He'd go to the zoo and take pictures of the animals; kangaroos and donkeys and goats, yellow eyes staring out of darkened paddocks.

I believed him, about the photographs, though I wondered about the explanation. I had crazy thoughts, that maybe there was nothing wrong with his film, but instead something wrong with that night. Then I found two of the photographs that supposedly hadn't come out. They were under the grate in our fireplace, scorched at the edges. One was a blurry shot taken up on the observation deck. It seemed to be one he'd snapped by accident, with the camera in motion so that most of the picture was a smudge, the stars falling like embers, the radome an enormous white blot consuming one entire side of the image. Right at the edge of the picture, though, was a woman, standing near the railing. Only part of her was visible, the edge of a fur coat, long, dark hair.

The other photograph was obviously one that he'd captured with the flash after the lights had all gone out. In the foreground were the fleshy shapes of panicked guests running in front of the camera, pushing and falling over each other in the darkness, but in the background was Henri, the focus on him perfect so that you could see the defeated expression on his unsmiling face. He stood in front of his "Chernobog" painting, looking out at the rioting crowd as though he could see them, his eyes vacant. Worse, though, than anything about his expression was something that I tried to tell myself was an optical illusion created by the effect of the flash and the angle. The hoof of the painting's black goat, resting on Henri's shoulder, beckoning him to turn and follow.

I kept the pictures, thumbed through them relentlessly, obsessively, wearing smeared fingerprints into the edges. I meant to confront Nicky with them, throw them down on the table, demand to know why he hadn't shown them to me, why he'd lied to me, burned the evidence. But instead I watched him, his new confidence, his new photographs. He made friends that I didn't know, went to parties and gallery openings that I declined to attend, staying home with a bottle in my hand. When he was gone I would take out the pictures, look at them again and again.

Finally, I waited for him to leave the apartment one night and I followed him. Watched him walk down the street, his head up, not slouching, not anymore, and saw him go to the corner and get into a cab with someone. A woman with long dark hair, wearing a fur coat.

AUTHOR'S NOTES:

Here's a secret: I had already started this story before I was aware that there was going to be a tribute anthology to Laird Barron, let alone before Ross Lockhart and Justin Steele had invited me to contribute something to *The Children of Old Leech*. I started writing "Walpurgisnacht" after reading Laird Barron's second—and still my favorite—collection, *Occultation*. I wanted to see what a Laird Barron story would look like if I wrote it.

When the invite to *The Children of Old Leech* came in, I dusted off the story and tuned it up. In writing "Walpurgisnacht," I tried to do something similar to what I do when I'm writing stories for Lovecraftian anthologies, which was to take more of the beats and themes of Laird's fiction, rather than copping too many of the names or specific stories, although "Something Scary" and real-life photographer Eadweard Muybridge both found their way in.

I also worked in some references to my *own* stories, and both the Steadman Gallery and its show on "The New Decadence" should sound familiar to those who've read my previous collection.

THE RED CHURCH

At first, Yvonne was happy to get the assignment. She'd been working for *The Current* for two months now, and hadn't gotten anything even remotely interesting. Art walks, First Fridays, gallery openings. Nothing juicy.

Wade Gorman was, if nothing else, juicy. He was a brilliant underground sculptor, or so the word went. He'd had a chance to go mainstream when the Sprint Center went up, was supposed to do something to commemorate the spot of the Union Prison Collapse just across the street that killed four women and injured dozens of others back in 1863, kicking off the Lawrence Massacre. The designs he turned in got him kicked off the commission. Yvonne couldn't find any good pictures of them online, but the blurry cell phone photos she did turn up looked like a sort of tower made of piled bodies, though whether those bodies were wrapped together in death or pleasure, she couldn't tell.

"Why would you even commission someone like Gorman for something like that?" she asked Dale one evening, spinning her laptop around on the kitchen counter to show him one of Gorman's sculptures, a variant on Saint Sebastian; bald, gray, and sunken-eyed, looking like a corpse from a plague pit, and impaled with dozens of lengths of rebar.

"The people who put that stuff together don't even know what he does," Dale said, leaning down to slide a pan of vegetables into

73

the oven. "They just tell their assistant, 'Give me someone hip, someone edgy,' and then when their assistant brings them a guy who sculpts stacked corpses, they chew his ass."

There was surprisingly little about Gorman on the Internet. She was able to find a few pictures of his early work, but nothing for at least the last six years. Her editor said he was still working, though, churning away in this building that he owned outright, that was his apartment and studio all in one. "New projects," her editor said. "Nobody's ever even seen them. It'll be an exclusive."

In more ways than one, she found, because Gorman had never, ever agreed to an interview before. Even when he got the commission and lost it, when the *Star* was hounding him for a piece, when even the national news syndicates had come down to try to talk to him, he'd turned everyone away with short, terse replies and "No comment"s.

Yvonne didn't ask her editor why now. She assumed that Gorman was planning some kind of comeback, and hoped to use the interview as a catapult. But more than that, she didn't actually care why. She was so damn sick of fluff pieces, so happy to get something she could at least sink her teeth into, that she didn't want to look too closely at the mouths of any gift horses.

Gorman didn't live in one of the nice lofts in the Crossroads, like most of the artists she knew. His building was farther downtown, and farther east. A brick two-story with a thick iron door and an electrical substation across the street, an old envelope factory next to that. There was nothing else on the block where Gorman's building sat, and the weeds in the vacant lots on either side grew taller than Yvonne, sporting unlikely purple flowers.

Her editor told her that Gorman didn't have a phone. She just had to go. "He's always there," her editor said. "Where the hell else would he be?" But the first time she went, she banged on the metal door for fifteen minutes to no avail. Upon first driving down, she'd assumed that the factory across the street was closed, maybe turned into lofts like all the others, but there were workers standing out on the loading dock smoking cigarettes. They watched her, and talked amongst themselves in quick, quiet bursts, but thankfully they didn't cross the street, didn't hoot or yell or whistle, even though she was wearing the black skirt that she knew showed off her ass. Eventually, she drove home and left a message on her editor's voicemail that Gorman hadn't been in.

She got a text message back saying, "Try again."

The next time she went by Gorman's building it was spitting rain out of a gray sky. She went on a Saturday, because maybe Gorman would be more likely to be home then. Maybe he secretly had to get a day job to support himself, since he wasn't selling any sculptures these days. Maybe he was even working across the street at the envelope factory.

She also figured that, on a Saturday, there wouldn't be anyone at the factory to watch her. But as she stood in the damp air and pounded the heel of her hand against the door, stepping from foot to foot because of the cold that bit with each gust of wind, she found herself wishing that they were back, because their stares and whispers were better than the barrenness that filled the place now.

Though she was constantly *aware* of the danger, she'd never felt unsafe in the city. She was always conscious of the proximity of so many other people, and it comforted her. The country was the place she couldn't abide, where emptiness stretched out around her like the cold vacuum of space. Here, though, standing outside of Gorman's building, she felt that same loneliness, felt cut off from all the souls that she knew inhabited the city in which she lived.

As she was thinking of that, the door suddenly disappeared from beneath her hand. She made a startled sound, a squeak, and was instantly annoyed with herself. It was, of course, just Gorman, towering in the now-open doorway. She took him in with a glance. There'd been the occasional picture in the papers, but they didn't capture him. Didn't capture his height, the distinctness of his moon-shaped head, his forehead and chin so prominent as to be called jutting, his eyes dark and small, like beads set in his face. His hands were big and strong-looking. *Sculptor's hands,* she wanted to think, but *strangler's hands* is what her mind supplied instead.

"The paper sent you?" he asked before she could speak. She nodded, then fumbled her notepad and held out her hand to shake.

He ignored her proffered hand, appraised her obviously with his gaze, not in a sexual way, she didn't think, not at all the way she was used to being appraised by men, but like he'd just been asked to judge the value of an antique clock, or the health of a stranger's horse.

"Watch your step," he said, disappearing back into the dark.

Just inside the metal door was a concrete hallway, bare and unlit except for what illumination straggled in from outside, and what fell down the metal stairs that Gorman was already halfway up by the time her eyes adjusted to the dimness. His footfalls were surprisingly quiet on the stairs, and she winced at each clang her own shoes made as she followed him.

The entire top floor was the studio. It was dark, drenched in shadow. Though the back wall was all windows, drapes were pulled closed across them, letting in only a shaft of gray light. Bare bulbs hung from the ceiling, but they seemed small and insignificant in the gloom of the place. Yvonne wondered how Gorman managed to work there at all.

But work he must, because the room was filled with pieces. She counted quickly as her eyes skimmed over them. She couldn't be sure, but she knew there had to be more than a dozen, all covered in white sheets, like the furniture in an old castle in some movie.

"Are these all recent works?" she asked, but he didn't respond. "What's your medium?" she tried again, but he simply waved his hand, as though her questions were of no importance. Yvonne shook her head, thinking that she was wasting her time, that this was going to be a very disappointing assignment after all. Then Gorman pulled the sheet off one of the figures in the middle of the studio.

In the red forest there is a red church

After that first meeting with Gorman, she had a dream. She was walking through what looked like a forest at night, only it also *didn't* look like a forest. The ground beneath her feet was as white and featureless as a sheet of paper, the night solid black and bereft of any star or cloud. The trees that grew up everywhere around her were red from trunk to tip. They appeared to be denuded of leaves, but their red branches split and split again until they became too small to see, until they became like a red cloud filling the air above her head.

***

She woke up in bed, Dale breathing easily beside her, and she realized that she couldn't remember the sculpture that Gorman had shown her. She tried to call it back to memory, but her mind kept playing tricks on her, replacing it with constellations of glowing light or masses of moving feathers. After he'd shown it to her she'd made her mumbled apologies, to which he had seemed almost pleased, as though this was the reaction he'd intended, and then she'd stumbled down the metal steps and, with their clangor still resounding in her ears, had been sick next to her Malibu.

When she'd looked up, there'd been two men standing across the street, next to the concrete wall around the substation, their hoods pulled up against the spattering rain, staring at her. They'd stood there, unmoving, until she'd wiped off her mouth and driven away.

It scared her that she couldn't remember the sculpture. The next morning, she drove down to the offices of *The Current* and sat at the curb with her engine running for twenty minutes, trying to work up the nerve to go in and tell her editor that, no, she wasn't going to be able to do this Gorman story. Or even a lie, that Gorman had refused the interview. In the end, she didn't do either, just drove away.

She didn't go back to Gorman's that day. She went out to lunch, even though it was barely ten, and then drove all the way down to the Plaza and walked around looking in windows until one o'clock. She kept telling herself that she was *going* to go to Gorman's, that she was just putting it off because he was an artist and they kept weird hours, that he probably wasn't even going to be awake before noon anyway. That excuse worked for awhile, and then she went to a movie, some light, romantic comedy that she barely remembered, something that was supposed to be funny but that she couldn't laugh at, and then she went back to the apartment before Dale got home. She ordered Chinese for dinner, and then was startled when the doorbell rang.

When Dale got home from work and asked how her day had gone, she found herself lying and telling him that Gorman hadn't been in when she went by. "He's probably trying to make himself seem mysterious," Dale said, and she just nodded.

Whatever she may have dreamed that night, she couldn't remember it upon waking.

***

The next day, she felt stupid about dodging work the day before. She drove first thing down to *The Current*, and made a big show about rooting around in her desk, picking up files, letting anyone who saw her know that she was on the job. Then she drove back over to Gorman's.

The factory was open again. It was a cold day, not raining this time, but windy enough that she clutched her notebook to her chest when she got out of the car. There was no one out on the loading dock smoking in the wind, but she felt eyes on her from the dark doorways, though she told herself that she was just being paranoid.

She beat her palm against Gorman's door and waited. At first there was no sound from the other side, just the dull echoes of her own poundings, and she worried that maybe she had pissed him off by not coming the day before. Had she said she would? She couldn't remember.

Then she heard a sound from the other side of the door. A far-off moaning, or a scraping, like something being dragged. The kind of sound a ghost might make in an old story. She leaned forward to press her ear to the door, just as it came open and Gorman was standing there. He reminded her, she realized as she whipped her head back, a little bit of Frankenstein's monster, with his jutting features and imposing height.

"You came back," he said, as though genuinely surprised to see her. "Good."

And then he was leading her up the stairs again, just walking away into the dark interior of the building, expecting her to follow.

The studio was different, she realized as soon as she crested the stairs. Everything had been moved around, and the pieces were no longer draped in their ghostly sheets. Her eyes skimmed them, skipping across each piece and waiting to take them in later, looking for the one she had seen on Saturday, the one she still couldn't remember, but none of them looked familiar.

"Are these…" she started to ask, but Gorman shook his head, gesturing around.

"Look at them first," he said. "Take your time."

So she did, walking from piece to piece, letting her gaze soak up all the details. Though they seemed natural extensions of Gorman's earlier work, still she'd never really seen anything like them. She'd gone to that Bodies Revealed exhibit with Dale when it came to Union Station, but these weren't like those.

She couldn't tell what they were made of, but they looked real. Human bodies, stripped of skin and exploded, so that their anatomies seemed to be bursting apart. Here was a head, the side flying off, one eye leaping forward, and a glowing lightbulb in the place where the brain should have been. There was a man whose ribcage swung open to reveal organs suspended on wires, like a macabre orrery. Each of them affixed all over with careful little paper squares bearing letters and numbers, figures from the Greek alphabet, and symbols she'd never seen before.

Of course they couldn't be real, she knew that, but they *looked* so real. She reached out to touch one, but her hand paused, hovering just over a suspended heart. "What are they?" she asked, without looking over her shoulder to where Gorman stood.

"Saints," Gorman replied. "Angels. Apostles. Boddhisatvas. They come to bring us the word, the light. They go before, to show us the way."

That wasn't really what she'd been asking. Not *What do they represent?* but *What are they made of?* Still, it made her remember that she was supposed to be interviewing, made her pull her hand back, fumble out her notepad, her pen.

Saints, she wrote on the otherwise blank yellow page. *Angels.*
In the red church there is a red altar

The next time she had the dream, she saw a building through the trees. It seemed strange to her, even in the dream, because the building and the trees were the same color, so how could she see it?

It was a wood-plank church, like the one they had in the town where she grew up, where she couldn't wait to move away. It had a little steeple and everything, except all the planks were as red as red could be. Maybe, she thought, they were cut from all these red trees, all sawed up.

In her dream, she walked up to the door of the church. It was black, not a door at all but a hole into the night sky, maybe, and as she stepped through it she felt so cold.

***

Dale woke up that time, followed her to the door of the bathroom where he stood rubbing his eyes while she let the water in the shower heat up. She wanted it hot enough to broil her, to bake her skin red.

"I'm worried about these dreams," he said, even though she hadn't told him about the dreams, not really. "You're not sleeping."

"I'm sleeping," she said as she stepped into the shower, but even as she said it she didn't know if it was true. She couldn't really remember how much sleep she *had* actually been getting.

When she'd gotten home from her second attempt at interviewing Gorman, Dale had asked her what his stuff was like. "Do you remember in *House on Haunted Hill*—the new one—when they go down into the basement? You remember those bodies in the glass cases? They're sort of like that," she'd said, even though, as time passed, she thought less and less that even that was quite right.

"Creepy," Dale had said, and she'd realized that, yeah, she guessed they were, but the sculptures weren't what scared her, not after that first session, anyway. What scared her was what she couldn't remember. She kept her notes carefully hidden from Dale, something that she'd never done before, because they scared her, too. They weren't like any interview notes she'd ever taken, and she couldn't remember writing them down. Couldn't remember what questions, if any, they were in answer to. Couldn't remember Gorman saying them at all.

They were just scrawls, the kind of notes she'd write if she were running out to catch a bus, and they said things like *Men of science turn their eyes toward the stars in the hopes of finding there the invisible gears that turn the universe, but you can't see the truth in the largest of things* and *The human body is a temple, it's true, but when we go to the temple, we don't worship out in the street, do we?*

***

When she went back the last time and pounded on Gorman's door, the clouds had gone away and the day was sunny, though a chilly breeze still scudded along the ground, blowing bits of trash and making the tall purple flowers in the vacant lot bob their heads. The men at the factory were standing out on the loading docks again, but this time she welcomed them, welcomed their tenuous connection to the life of the city she usually felt all around her, but from which she felt strangely severed here.

She struck the door three times, and on the third blow it simply swung open, like the front door of some haunted manor in a bad movie. She stepped inside and called Gorman's name up the stairs, but he didn't answer. She stood at the bottom, uncertain, and for a moment she considered walking down the cinderblock hallway, seeing what was on the bottom floor of the building. *Probably nothing,* she had always told herself before. *Boarded-up storefronts or whatever.* But today, standing there without a guide, she was suddenly curious.

She strained her ears, listening for any hint of movement, any indication that Gorman was waiting for her at the top of the stairs, that he might descend at any moment and catch her in her trespass. All she heard was a low, distant hum, coming from down the dark hallway.

She didn't follow it. She took a step in that direction, two, and then she looked up at the top of the stairs again, at the doorway there. She could imagine Gorman standing silently in it, watching her with his moon-face, and she shook her head and ascended the stairs instead.

Gorman wasn't there. She looked in every corner, behind every sculpture. She pushed aside the drapes that blocked off his cot, and peered into the bathroom, but he wasn't anywhere to be found.

On her second visit, she'd pulled out a camera and tried to snap some photos, but Gorman had stopped her, held his hand in front of the lens and shaken his big head slowly back and forth, as though he was disappointed in her. "These aren't ready to be shown," he'd said.

But he wasn't there now, and she pulled the camera out of her bag and began taking pictures of the sculptures, hurriedly, furtively. The lighting was bad so she had to use the flash, and every time she raised her face from the viewfinder, every time her eyes adjusted to the light, she expected to see him standing there, ready to admonish her, to snatch the camera from her and smash it on the concrete floor, she wasn't sure what. But he never appeared.

Her illicit photography made her feel giddy, and when she ran out of space on her memory card she stumbled to the stairs and down them, her shoes clattering on the metal steps. As she reached the bottom, a sound came from down the dark hall at her back that stopped her in place, froze her blood. A moan. Not ghostly this time, not the sound of an unused door, but a gurgling, pleading sound. A sound that had blood in it, and pain.

She ran.

Outside, the day was still blustery, still sunny, but the men at the factory had disappeared. There was nothing anywhere that told her that the city she stood in the middle of was inhabited at all, anything but a carcass now, bereft of whatever life it had once possessed. Far off in the distance she could track what she thought was a single car moving along an overpass, but it might have been her imagination, or a trick of the light. For the first time in her life the idea struck her that maybe the city was empty, that all the windows looked in onto cobwebs and dust.

She got in her car and drove until she saw people.

Later on, she explained the moan she'd heard a million ways. Guilty conscience, overactive imagination, the wind. And even if it had been a human voice, as some tiny, inside part of her knew it had, then there were a hundred reasons for it, reasons that were none of her business, that she was better off leaving unexplored.

She went to the office late, after she was sure that her editor and anyone who knew her would be gone, and pulled up the photos on her computer. As she scrolled through them she expected, as each new image materialized, to see Gorman there, hidden by shadows, just the edge of his profile illuminated by the camera's flash. But he never appeared. Just his sculptures, their details painted in exquisite relief, every vein, every ridge of muscle preserved, captured. *They're so real*, she found herself thinking as she printed off the best of the pictures.

But they couldn't be real, could they?

And upon the red altar there is a red knife

Inside, the church was bigger than it had appeared from without. The walls were vaulted, and they alternated stripes of black and red. It was, she decided, like being in the belly of a whale, like in *Pinocchio*, as she watched the walls expand and contract, expand and contract, as though with breath.

There were scattered pews on either side of her, and ahead, where the altar and the cross would have been in the church back home, there hung a huge heart, suspended in the air and connected to the walls and ceiling by a network of branches, all beating in time to the expansion and contraction of the walls.

***

When she woke up, she slipped out of bed as slowly as she could, so as not to wake Dale, then locked herself in the bathroom and looked through the photos again. She'd taped one to her notepad, a picture of a torso with its chest removed, its innards spilling out, its organs floating up from it on wires. Beneath it she had written—in dark, repeated strokes—*This is a map of the universe.*

Of course, she couldn't remember writing it.

The next day, after she kissed Dale goodbye when he left for work, she sat at the computer and read about Gunther von Hagens and his plastination method, which had yielded up the Bodies Revealed exhibit that she and Dale had attended, and others all over the world. She looked at picture after picture of human bodies, plasticized and exploded, and she held the photos she'd taken in Gorman's studio up next to the screen. Gorman's were different, yes. Different in tone, different in style. But in detail, in execution?

She shook her head. No way. No way he'd been plasticizing real people, real bodies, and no one had heard about it.

There was a lot to read about von Hagens, and her searches also led her to the wax anatomical sculptures of Gaetano Giulio Zumbo and to images from the vaults of the Hunterian museum, with circulatory systems shellacked to wooden doors. Before she knew it, darkness had fallen outside the apartment and rain was slashing against the windows. Thunder boomed and rattled the glass, and she looked up to see that her phone showed that she'd missed a call. It was set on vibrate, but she'd been so absorbed in the macabre images she hadn't seen it light up, hadn't noticed it moving.

She picked it up, clicked over. It was Dale's number, but the voicemail, when she listened to it, wasn't any words at all, just a rasping, choking sound, and then terrible silence.

As little as two days earlier, and she would have called the police. It would have been her first thought. She would have tried Dale back and, when he didn't answer, dialed his work, and then the police. But not that night. That night she just ran, leaving the computer open to a picture of a flayed man on a flayed horse, leaving her notebook open to the last page where she'd written *Where is the red church?* Ran out into the rain to her car, and from there drove to where she knew, knew in her guts and in her bones, the call had come from.

***

She tried to call Dale three times on the way over, but the phone just rang and rang until voicemail picked it up. Each time she heard his voice telling her to leave a message, her heart jumped, thinking she was wrong, thinking he was okay after all, and then it sank again, deeper each time.

When she parked in front of Gorman's building, the phone still pressed to her ear, rining once more, Dale's voice telling her again to leave a message and he'd get back to her, she slammed the door and stood in the rain for a minute. Her hair was soaked, spilling water down her back. She stared at the metal door, wondered if it would open this time, wondered what she'd do if it didn't.

But it did, it pushed open under her silent touch, just as it had before; as if the building was abandoned, no one home. But as she stepped inside, above the thunder of the rain pounding against the walls and the roof, she could hear a distant sound. The ringing of the phone against her ear, and the answering chime, the song they'd danced to at the Drum Room on their second anniversary, coming tinnily from down the dark hall ahead of her.

No light filtered down from upstairs, none worth mentioning came in through the door that hung half-open at her back. The hallway was dark as pitch. She hung up, and held her phone up in front of her, lighting her way.

The door at the other end was painted red, something she'd never noticed before as it'd always been lost in shadows. It was metal, like the front door, and when she rested her hand against it she found it warm to the touch, as though the heater was on full blast on the other side. There was a smell, too, not like blood, or not like what she thought of as being like blood, but a hot, moist smell, like the reptile house at the zoo.

The door had a place for a padlock, but it was gone. Just a metal latch held it closed now, and she knew, somewhere in the back of her mind, in the part that remembered watching scary movies, that she shouldn't go in there, that it was a trap, that something terrible and irrevocable was waiting on the other side of that door for her and that all she had to do to survive was to run, run now, run away, and everything would be fine.

But of course it wouldn't be fine. She was too far into the movie for that. Leaving now, she was just delaying it, making it worse. What was behind that door, whatever it was, it was her fault, somehow. She knew that now. It was her bed, she'd made it, and now all that was left was to step inside and lie in it.

She opened the door.

Take the red knife and cut red bread!

Yvonne had never been in a slaughterhouse, so she couldn't

compare the smell of the room to one. It smelled like snakes to her, like terrariums and like the red, watery blood that used to pool in the bottoms of the Styrofoam containers of meat that her mother brought home from the grocery store.

The room was lit by old-fashioned fixtures set in the wall. They made a low buzzing, and at first she thought that's what she'd heard when she almost went down the hall earlier. But no. Not them. Flies.

There weren't that many of them, the ones that slipped in when the doors opened, the ones that crept in through tiny cracks in the building, but there were enough. They buzzed from place to place, settling on the black streaks of dried blood, settling on the bodies that hung from the wall in front of her.

What had she imagined she would find? Mad science labs from old movies? A surgical suite, laid out for plasticizing bodies like the ones upstairs? No, those weren't the bodies. Those were just sculptures, expertly done. Just practice. Gorman's voice, "These aren't ready to be shown." Here was the real thing. Bodies laid open, organs pulled out. Hearts still beating, lungs still pumping. Heads looking from side to side, eyes blank, gray. Breath whispering in and out in soft little moans and gasps. How did he do it? How were they still alive?

She scanned their faces, willing herself not to count them, willing herself not to feel guilty when she breathed just that much easier when she saw that Dale's face wasn't among them. Then, her phone buzzing in her hand, Dale's number flashing up on her display, and from the shadows a movement, tall and moon-faced, and the flash of a knife.

Ten years in the city, and she'd always felt safe. But her father felt safe in the country, in the small towns where they'd lived, and he still kept a gun under the front seat of his truck. She'd taken self-defense courses for six of those ten years, and while they had mostly taught her how to avoid bad situations, how to look confident, to keep her cell phone handy, they'd also taught her how to use an attacker's superior weight against him, how to turn a knife blade, how to break a wrist.

The knife clattered to the concrete floor as Gorman stumbled past her, nearly colliding with his own pieces, his own sacred relics. By the time he turned around the knife was already in her hand, and then it was in his stomach, turning, sliding up, and he was choking on blood.

If it had happened even a week earlier, it probably would have ended there. As it was, she carved and carved until Dale went on a break at work and noticed his cellphone missing. Until he called her to see if he'd left it at the apartment and got no answer. Until he drove home and found her gone, found her notes beside the computer. Until he called her editor and her editor called the police, who found her, bloodied and smiling, in the midst of the sculpture that had once been Wade Gorman. "He's a saint," she kept repeating as they dragged her away. "An angel."

AUTHOR'S NOTES:

"The Red Church" was the third of my stories to appear in a Word Horde anthology, following on the heels of "Ripperology" and "Walpurgisnacht." And while I wrote it for Ross Lockhart's *Giallo Fantastique*, at the time I first started working on the story, I hadn't actually seen very many *Giallo* films, though I *had* been doing a lot of reading about them.

Known to most as the Italian ancestors of the modern slasher film, what I love about *Gialli* aren't the justly-famous kill sequences, but the sense of menace and strangeness that the best of them carry in every note and every frame. Because I hadn't seen many of them when I wrote it, "The Red Church" is probably inspired less directly by any particular *Giallo* than it is by their spirit, and by a variety of other sources. The title and the verses that break up the tale are all from Albertus Magnus, though I first came to them by way of Manly Wade Wellman. The images of the bodies pulled apart come from my obsession with wax anatomical models, and from Mike Mignola's drawings of same.

This is another Kansas City story, and is set right near where I was working at the time that I wrote it, though I took some liberties with the geography. The Union Prison Collapse is actual history, though in real life there's just a sign up on the corner to commemorate it.

REMAINS

Mostly I remember the room. The way it smelled. The dank, sullen darkness, hot and thick with closed-up summertime sweat. I remember the voice of the round-faced little guy the parents had gotten to preside over the thing. Not a priest, not technically, but someone who was willing to do the job.

I don't know why that's what always sticks in my mind, rather than what came later, after all hell broke loose. I never wanted to be doing anything like that ever again, but when Jenny asked for my help I couldn't say no. Not after what she'd been through. Not when she told me why.

***

The house we pull up in front of is one of *those* houses. Dark and sullen, like the room. If it was a kid, you'd take one look at it and say that it'd been abused.

I flick my cigarette out the window onto the wet pavement, and try not to think too hard about why we're here, but I do anyway. I wonder if the house would look the way it does to me if I didn't know its history. If I was just walking by on the street, would I give it a second glance?

It's a big house, and it was nice once, but it's sat for awhile now in disrepair, untenanted. It belonged to Dr. Terrence Kinter, who lived in it for almost forty years, during which time he killed over four dozen kids. No one's really sure how many. When the police finally caught him they found hundreds of bones buried in his garden and under the floorboards of the house. Little tiny bones.

While he was still alive he worked at the hospital up on the hill as a "consulting physician" for awhile before he retired. His neighbors all thought he was eccentric but benign. After his arrest, several people were shown on the news saying things like, "He seemed like such a nice old man."

When he was arrested he didn't come easy. He fought two officers, gouged out one's eye and bit off the other's ear. They had to beat him pretty bad before they were finally able to get him cuffed.

He never made it to trial, but it wouldn't have mattered much, I don't think, because he started admitting his crimes as soon as they had him in custody. Admitting them, and all sorts of other things. He said he was a sorcerer, and talked at length about casting enchantments to lure kids to his house, and about the things he'd conjured up and fed with their hearts.

A lot of people wanted him to fry. Figuratively speaking, of course, since we had lethal injection. Jenny was one of them. She'd have happily killed him herself, if an embolism in his brain hadn't beaten her to it only two days after he was arrested.

That was over a year ago, and since then her only consolation's been that at least her son was the last of Dr. Kinter's victims. Until now.

In the last two weeks, two kids have disappeared from this same neighborhood. No trace. Nothing. Officially, it's nothing. Missing persons still, not even the business of homicide, not yet. And definitely nothing to do with Kinter, who's been dead and in the ground for a year and change, case closed.

But Jenny heard about it, about the kids, and she remembered Kinter, and this house, and so she called me. We'd been partners for awhile, back when I was still on the force, and we kept in touch. She'd heard about the exorcism, she knew that I'd, well, maybe not *believe* her, but at least humor her. At least go with her.

She was right.

So here I am, standing out in the damp afternoon, looking up at Kinter's old house that's been empty all this time, because who wants to live in *that* house, you know? It's going to be bulldozed, one of these days, and they're going to put something else up here. A Ronald McDonald House, they talked about, which seems kind of like a bad idea to me.

"Jenny," I say, and she pulls her eyes off the house and looks at me. She looks excited and scared, like she's sitting in the seat of a roller coaster just as it crests the top of the big dive and maybe she wishes she hadn't gotten on in the first place. "What are we expecting to find in here?"

She shakes her head. "I don't know," she says. "Do you think ghosts... I mean do ghosts..." But she doesn't know what she means, and she just trails off.

"I don't know anything about ghosts," I tell her. "I don't know anything about anything. What I want to tell you is, probably, we're not going to find one damned thing in there. You know that, right? This is probably a wild goose chase?"

She nods, and I can see that, while she's trying to believe it, she doesn't, not really. "I've got to see," she says.

"I know that. I understand. I just need you to be prepared."

She nods again, and we start up the front steps.

The door's got a padlock on it. Bolted on and obviously newer than the wood it's attached to, but Jenny has a key that she got from somewhere, I don't ask how. She unlocks it, pushes it open, and we go in.

Inside, it doesn't look very much like a house anymore. The floorboards have been torn up in so many places, exposing the dark dirt underneath. It's hard to look at that dirt and not see makeshift graves; finger bones and eyeless sockets poking up. Accusing.

The furniture's been shoved aside, piled into corners to accommodate the excavation of the floors. A wall's been torn out between the entryway and the living room.

Only the shape of the place makes it still seem like a house, the walls still standing upright, making rooms that are just jumbles of displaced furniture and gaping wounds in the floor.

"Christ," Jenny says. She's never been in here before, any more than I have. They wouldn't let her be involved in the investigation. She puts her hand to her mouth, and if I'm imagining the graves dug under the floor, picturing the bones hidden down there, then I can only guess what she must be imagining.

I put my hand on her back. "I'm okay," she says around her hand, then lowers it to her side. "I'm okay."

The entryway lets into the living room on one side, and a sort of parlor on the other. There's a piano in the parlor with one of its legs broken off. This stuff was all slated for sale, everything that was left in the house, but the public outrage over Kinter's crimes delayed it, and then it just got forgotten, I guess.

In the living room is a huge fireplace that must be the structural center of the house, its base sinking into the ground and the bricks of its chimney extending up beyond the roof.

Beside the fireplace is a picture on the wall, though all the others are gone. It's not a big one, just a sepia-toned photograph. It shows Dr. Kinter sitting and staring straight at the camera. He's already an old man in the picture, for all its apparent age. The way he's dressed is as old-fashioned as the picture looks; a top hat and tails, with his knobby hands folded on the head of a cane. His eyes look tiny and black and seem to catch some light from outside the frame, glinting like the eyes of a doll, or the eyes of a shark.

"That's him," Jenny says, walking over to get a closer look at the picture. Her next move is so sudden that it startles me. She grabs the photo off the wall and hurls it, gilt-frame and all, across the room like a discus. I flinch as it hits the far wall and shatters, glass tinkling to the floor.

Jenny takes a deep breath, shuddering, like someone who's been held under water too long. "I'm sorry," she says. "It's harder than I expected."

"You don't have to do this," I tell her. "I can look around. You know I'll tell you if I find anything."

"No," she says, and then reaches out a hand without looking and lays it on my arm, giving it a squeeze. "No, I'm okay. But thank you. For coming. For everything."

I pat her hand. I'm keeping my own hands from shaking, but only by trying very hard. I don't want to set her on edge any more than I know she already is, but the place is getting to me. I want very badly to draw the pistol out of my shoulder holster, but I content myself with shifting so that I can feel it against me, reminding me that it's there.

Not that it'll necessarily do me any good. I've never heard of any ghost stories where guns were terribly effective.

"Should we look upstairs?" Jenny asks. I nod and she heads out of the living room, keeping close to the wall to avoid the hole in the floor.

The stairs are still intact, and they squeak under us as we go up. The rooms there look more like real rooms, though all the accoutrements are gone. Just beds and chairs and an empty trunk. The only unpleasantness is a bedroom with an exterior lock on the door, and little child-sized furniture inside. It's nothing Jenny and I aren't expecting—we followed the investigation, after all—but it still causes us both to recoil, like from a bad smell.

We're standing at the top of the stairs, and I'm watching Jenny's face, watching her start to accept that there's nothing here, that these two kids don't have anything to do with Kinter, don't have anything to do with her son, and that she's only torturing herself by being here, and I'm trying to decide whether to say anything to her or whether to let her process it at her own speed, when there's a sound from the chimney. A dragging, scuffling, thumping sound, like something got caught in there and can't get out. Then something else, a thud, and then a sound like bare, heavy footsteps on the boards downstairs.

Jenny is already moving before I can reach for my pistol, taking the stairs two at a time. The pounding of her feet on the steps drowns out any other sound I might hear, and I can't do anything but draw my gun and follow her. She careens around the corner, into the living room, and I see that she's got her gun out, too, and then she says, "Shit," and she's gone again.

I get to the living room a bit behind her, and she's already past it into the dining room. I see what she saw, that the living room's empty, but I also see what she missed, that the photo's back on the wall.

The glass is still broken out, bits of it hanging in the bent frame like ragged teeth, but it's been hung back up. By a human hand, I wonder, or a ghostly one?

I start to go over to it, I don't know why, to take it back down before she sees it maybe, when there's a godawful crash like a rockslide from the dining room and a startled noise and a curse and two gunshots and I run around the fireplace after the sound.

For a second I don't see Jenny. When I do, she's lying in the dirt below the dining room floor, her gun gripped in both hands and held straight out ahead of her. She's staring at a big hole in the side of the chimney, and there are bricks and pieces of bricks scattered all over what's left of the floor.

I drop down into the hole, but I don't touch her. She looks like she might shoot me if I did, without even knowing she was doing it.

"What happened?" I ask instead, trying to keep my voice level while also keeping the hole in the chimney in my peripheral vision.

"I don't," she says, but that's it, then her mouth just works uselessly and no words come out.

"It's okay," I say, and she shakes her head wildly, jerking her chin at the hole in the chimney.

"It came out of there."

"What?" I ask, turning my gaze more fully to the hole.

She shakes her head, like she couldn't possibly put a name to it, and finally just says, "A monster."

***

We go back out to the cars and stand, staring up at the house. We've got our guns put away so that nobody driving past will call the cops on us, but they're not far from our thoughts.

"What was it like?" she asks, leaning on her car for support, and I know she's talking about the exorcism. She heard about it, but not from me. She's never asked me about it before; we've never really talked it over.

"I don't know," I tell her, truthfully. "I saw things. I know they were real, but I don't know what they were, not really, and I can't describe them. If I did, they wouldn't sound like much, they wouldn't come out right. I know that."

"How'd you deal with it?" she asks, and I think about the long nights when even the sleeping pills don't help, about the fights with Maggie and about finally coming home one day and finding all her stuff gone.

"I really didn't," I reply.

She nods, chewing her lower lip. "It was big," she finally says. "Bigger than a person. Like an ape, maybe, but it didn't seem like it was finished. I don't know if that's the right way to say it or not. It seemed like a person in a bag or something, so that the shape was right, but there weren't any details. Arms, legs, hands. No eyes. Just a mouth. A big mouth, with one big tooth like a knife right in the middle of it, nothing else."

She stops, and I don't know what to say so I don't say anything. "I put two rounds in it and it went up the chimney," she says. "Do you think... is that what a ghost is, do you think? Was that him?"

I shake my head. "I don't know what a ghost is. I don't know anything about ghosts. But I don't think it was him."

She looks down at the ground, and when she speaks it's really soft. "I don't think it was either."

***

We talk for a while, awkwardly, badly, about what we should do. What we're going to do. Finally I convince her to go, that I'll call the police, say that a client had me doing unrelated surveillance work and I saw someone going into the old house. I'll tell them he was armed. That'll be enough for them to send out a couple of cars. I convince her that this isn't something we can, or should, do alone.

She's still in shock from whatever she saw, or I probably wouldn't be able to convince her of any of it.

She gets into her car and I get into mine. I pull out my cell phone and mime making the call, and she watches me through the windshield, and finally she pulls away from the curb. I watch until I can't see her car anymore, then I click my phone shut, turn my car off, and get out.

It's not that I don't think she could do what I'm going to do. She could, and maybe even better. But she shouldn't have to. I think about all those things I thought about before, the sleepless nights and the nightmares and Maggie and all of it, and I head back into the house.

Inside, nothing looks different. I walk around the hole in the living room floor and up to the fireplace. *"I put two rounds in it and it went up the chimney."* I take a deep breath, and then I stick my arm up into the fireplace, angling my pistol and firing once, twice. Then I jump back.

I don't have to wait long. There's a sound from up the chimney, a roar, then a slurping, bumping, sliding, scuffling noise, and then something comes half-falling, half-pouring out of the hearth, big and black and awful, like a sack full of wriggling tar. It pushes a stink out ahead of it, rotting weeds and hair left too long down a drain, and then it comes out mouth-first, that one huge tooth pointed straight at me like a dagger.

I fire into the thing as it's coming for me, and the bullets plow through it, throwing black slop at the walls, and it roars again but doesn't stop.

I step backward without meaning to, and there's no floor there behind me, and I'm falling down, and the thing is coming down on me like someone throwing a stinking black tarp over me. The smell is overpowering, and when the thing touches me it leaves a cold, clammy feeling, and something else. An impression, an idea, a picture in my mind's eye.

I shoot past the thing this time, aiming for the photo on the wall, trying to buy some time to think. The bullet hits, punches right through the middle of the picture, erasing the doctor's face.

The thing makes a sound almost like a wounded dog, and it recoils back from me for a second, like it's torn between attacking me and tending to the photo, and I take the time to scramble back to my feet.

The thing is still stuck halfway between the floorboards and the ground, indecisive, and when it sees me moving it lets out a wheezing shriek and rushes toward me. It comes at me with that tusk in its mouth, and instead of shooting I drop my gun and grab the tooth with both hands, stopping it from jabbing into my neck and twisting, jerking, tearing it out of the black mass. There's another horrible smell, worse than before, and then the thing shrinks up on itself like plastic cooking in a fire, and what drops from my hand is a normal human tooth.

I stand there for a breath, then another. I look down at the tooth where it lays in the dirt, and I notice that it seems like it's wriggling, rocking back and forth, trying to bury itself like a seed. I choke, and I want to leave, to run, but instead I drop down into the space under the floorboards and pick the tooth up with the fabric of my sleeve and drop it into my pocket.

***

And that's it. Or nearly it. I go back out to my car and call the police and tell them more or less what I told Jenny I would. I don't bother to claim that I saw someone going in, and I don't bother to say that he was armed. Just that I saw movement in the house, and maybe they should check it out.

The officers they send find the bodies of the two missing kids stuffed up the chimney. There's an investigation, of course, there has to be, and nothing I could possibly tell them would change that, so I don't tell them much of anything.

The only person I tell anything to is Jenny. I tell her that I'm sorry, and then I tell her what happened, and what I *think* happened. I tell her about what I saw when that thing touched me: Dr. Kinter, struggling with the police. A sharp blow across his mouth and a tooth knocked free of its moorings and spat into the fireplace.

She asks me if I think he did it on purpose, if he meant for the tooth to turn into that thing, and I tell her that I don't know. Maybe it was that, a last spell, or maybe something of his spirit still inhabited the tooth, or maybe it was something else entirely, something that we don't and can't and won't ever understand.

I tell her that I threw the tooth into the river, but I didn't. I thought about it, but then I imagined that thing crawling up from somewhere downstream, and instead I just dropped the tooth into a glass bottle, put the cork in really tight, and left it on my mantel.

There it sits, just a harmless tooth. I don't think it'll ever be anything else again. I don't think it would ever climb out if I did throw it in the river. Whatever made it into that thing, whatever gave it that terrible impetus, I think it was at least partly the fault of that house, and I can't help but wonder what would happen if you dug up the rest of Dr. Kinter's bones and dragged them back there.

AUTHOR'S NOTES:

There's a funny story that goes along with this one: It was originally called "The Tooth," and it was supposed to go into my first collection, *Never Bet the Devil & Other Warnings*. Just before it went to print, though, another author, who also happened to have a collection coming out with the same publisher at the same time, released a comic book called *The Tooth* that was about—believe it or not— a wizard's tooth that turned into a monster. Obviously, neither of us was familiar with the other's story, but it was too close for my publisher's comfort, and so "The Tooth" was pulled from the collection, and renamed "Remains" just for good measure. (I think it's a better title anyway, so I kept it.)

It later made an appearance in the special "lost" thirteenth issue of *Strange Aeons* that was available as a backer reward for the 2014 H. P. Lovecraft Film Festival Kickstarter, but has otherwise remained out of print.

The idea of using a previous supernatural experience to make a character better able to deal with their current predicament is one I really like, and I've toyed with it before. I think I first saw it done in Clive Barker's "The Last Illusion," which obviously informed my deployment of it here.

THE LABYRINTH OF SLEEP

Beyond the wall, the first moon has already risen. Kendrick stands still for a while, getting used to the changes to air, to gravity. He can still taste the last bitter dregs of the cigarette he stubbed out just before hooking up to the machine, can still smell the antiseptic tinge of the room he's left behind, as a breeze perfumed by distant and unnamed glades carries it away.

Down below him, at the bottom of the hill, is a forest of tall white trees, and beyond that the beginning of the Labyrinth. He's been here before, maybe not *right* here, but near enough. He's seen this moon before, stood under its light. He's been in that forest, even if maybe some other part of it. He's seen the split-headed giants that live there, the doors that they build in the ground, the men with cloven hooves and the heads of dogs, the black shapes that occasionally flit in front of the moon. All of this is familiar to him, but something about the night, *this* night, feels different. A smell in the air, like the ozone smell before a storm. Something.

Maybe it's because this trip *is* different. Not some hapless dreamer he's riding in this time but another rider, another professional. McCabe, lying in a drugged coma in his hotel room. McCabe, a few milligrams of noxitol short of dead, lying there on his bed, hooked up to monitors and IVs and to the machine. McCabe, waiting somewhere in the Labyrinth for Kendrick to come in and find him, to learn why he'd gone to the needle instead of his oldest friend.

The company is paying for the hotel room now, for the monitors, and paying Kendrick double his usual rate, but this one he'd do for free. He has to know what happened, what changed. Or, the worse answer, if nothing has, if this was always what waited at the end of McCabe's street and he's just been blind to it until now.

One way or the other, he has to know, and so he starts down the hill, toward the Labyrinth.

***

It probably started with the drugs, the new kinds of sleep aids to help a world full of light and motion find the time to dream. But it was the machine that ultimately did the job, that brought the wall of sleep crashing down. And what we found on the other side wasn't what we had expected, not at all. Not a changing jungle of Freudian symbols, not personal, not subjective. An actual place, the Labyrinth and the lands that surrounded it.

It took the machine to find it. The dreamers themselves never remembered somehow that they all went to the same place. On their trips back to consciousness the details of the dream world were lost, their minds replacing them with the minutiae of their memories and their own imaginations, the things that they remembered as their dreams. Always keyed to events in the Labyrinth, but never identical to it.

The machine was the silver key. With it, another person, a rider, could piggyback in on the dreamer's trip to that secret world. Not asleep, not really, and therefore not subject to the forgetfulness that true dreaming entailed.

It became a fad, a drug, an industry. In the waking world, there were dream parlors in every mall, where you could hook into someone's sleeping mind and take a ride to the Labyrinth. But most people were nothing more than tourists in the dreamlands, children stumbling along the turns of the Labyrinth. Kendrick and McCabe, they were professionals.

Or they had been, before McCabe tried to make himself sleep forever.

***

The walls of the Labyrinth are always black. Basalt, or something that can pass for it, the dreamland equivalent. They always rise up too high to scale, too high to jump. Once you're in the Labyrinth, you're in it, submerged, blind to anything except the next corner, and then the next.

Countless efforts have been made to map it. Kendrick has never known a professional who didn't have at least one in-progress map tacked up somewhere. But no one has ever managed. You can't see the Labyrinth from anywhere except the top of the hill, near the wall, and from there it all looks the same, and once you're in it, well…

There are landmarks. Some have been seen by more than one person. He and McCabe had compared their lists late one night. They'd both seen the fountain choked with moss. They'd both seen the doorway in the middle of the courtyard, the ground on the other side of it darker than on this side, but neither of them had been brave or stupid enough to step through. Kendrick had once seen a river, miles down, that cut a roaring chasm through the midst of the Labyrinth. McCabe claimed to have found a building that looked like an abandoned mosque, with no one inside but an altar set in the back with some kind of mummy in an alcove behind it, one he couldn't quite make out without getting closer than he suddenly found himself wanting to.

Some people say that the Labyrinth changes, and certainly Kendrick has never known two pros whose maps ever really lined up. Most people have an opinion on the subject, once they've put a few beers in themselves at the end of the day, but Kendrick never really thought about it before. To him, the Labyrinth was what it was. It was always there, on the other side of the wall, and it was always the same, really. Even if the paths changed, its nature never did, and that was enough for him.

$$***$$

He stands at one of the gates to the Labyrinth. All the gates he's ever seen looked identical. No horn or ivory, just unadorned clefts in the sides of the Labyrinth. Others have tried to mark them, he knows, but the markings were always gone when they came back. Either that, or no one has ever gone to the same gate twice.

It should be impossible, what he's doing. Going into a place that can't be mapped, to find someone who's been lost there already. It should be, but it never is. Something's different about the dreamers, maybe, or about the pros. Something in how they approach the Labyrinth, or in how it approaches them, but he's never gone in after a dreamer, never once, and not found them.

It isn't by any conscious art that he does it, though, at the same time, he knows it's not something everyone can do. He walks the Labyrinth as blind as if he were a dreamer himself. No one really knows how the professionals do it, the dream hounds, the *oneiroi*, as some in the industry have tried to dub them, though the name never stuck. Kendrick has his theories, all the pros do. To him, it's all in the thinking. Dreamers don't think while they're in the Labyrinth, not really. They can't. They're caught up in the black, forgetful rivers of sleep. But the riders, those who follow them in, *can* think, and, by thinking, by keeping their minds on their quarry, they can track them down. Whether that's by changing the turnings of the Labyrinth itself, or simply by knowing which way to turn their own steps, Kendrick doesn't know, and has never bothered to care.

Though time has no meaning here, still he knows that this is the longest he's ever been under. Out of the corners of his eyes, he sees what might be landmarks down curving paths, but already his feet are carrying him in another direction. He wonders how much time has passed out there in the waking world. It could be hours, minutes, days. They were prepared before he went under. IVs to feed and hydrate him, so that he could stay down no matter how long it took.

How long will they let him stay? How long before they pull the plug, before they decide that this errand is costing more than it's worth? He wills himself to hurry.

There are things that live in the Labyrinth. He's always known it. Not the giants or the dog-headed men or any of the other things that live outside. These are different, he knows, even though he's never seen them. He hears them sometimes, their hopping, shuffling gait just on the other side of a wall, just a few turns away. Sometimes in the waking world he tries to picture them, to imagine them as he goes about his day. He always sees them as pale, eyeless things, adapted to a life lived deep underground, though, of course, the Labyrinth is always open to the perpetual twilight of the dreamlands' sky.

When he's here, in the Labyrinth, he tries not to think of them at all, because he believes that thinking here has power. Even now, as he hears them behind him, he tries to think only of putting the next foot in front of him, then the next. Of going faster, not of why. Even when they sound like they are right behind him, just around the next turn, not even that far. That if he turned his head he would see them, see them at last as they are and not as he imagines. Even then he keeps his eyes forward, keeps his thoughts only on McCabe, McCabe, McCabe.

And then he turns a corner and he's somewhere he's never been before. Normally in the Labyrinth he can't say that, not with certainty. Most of it looks the same, excepting the occasional landmarks. But this is something else entirely. More than a landmark. This is *the* landmark. He knows it without even having to look around, knows even before his mind has processed what he's seen, knows with the faultless logic that is sometimes the province of the dreamlands, that this is the center of the Labyrinth.

The things behind him are forgotten, and, as if they are driven back by some invisible barrier, or as if it really has been his attention, however indirect, that held them here, the sounds of their pursuit cease. Or, was it ever really pursuit? Were they herding him here?

What would he call the structure that he sees before him, this extruded building of green stone with its soaring towers and many gaping windows, if he saw it in the waking world? A castle, a tower, a house?

There have been countless attempts to map the Labyrinth, and even more to explain it. Is it the first step of an afterlife, a tiny taste of death that we get each night when we close our eyes? Is it a representation of something from the collective unconscious, an enormous symbol housed in all our psyches? Is it a literally just the maze of our own neurons? These were things Kendrick never thought about, not outside the Labyrinth and certainly not within it, but he thinks about them now.

What does it mean, this structure? No map of the Labyrinth has ever found its center. No rider, no dream hound has ever come this far and returned, at least, not that he's ever heard of. In the mind of every sleeping man and woman, a maze, and in the center of the maze, this place. And inside this building, he knows with that same faultless logic, McCabe.

Without hesitating any further, he goes through the front door.

***

Inside, the house is *like* a castle, though strangely sparse and unfurnished. There are no guttering torches in sconces on the wall, but it isn't dark, either. The green stone seems to provide its own illumination.

When he passes windows and looks outside, what he sees isn't the Labyrinth, and that doesn't surprise him. Out one window massive stormclouds gather into an anvil-shaped thunderhead, crackling with multihued lightning. Out another, he looks down upon a misty valley, where golden statues nestled in peaks watch some kind of gladiatorial game on the distant floor below.

He walks here as he walked in the Labyrinth, one foot in front of the other, keeping his mind focused always on McCabe. This house isn't separate from the Labyrinth, he knows. It's part of it, maybe the greatest part, and here, more than ever, he must be very careful.

He tries to clear his mind of expectations, and so he is surprised when he suddenly stops walking. He's standing in the doorway to a room. At first glance it's not different than any of the other rooms he's passed, but then it is. It's furnished, with a fireplace and a single high-backed chair, and the window in the far wall is covered with a thick, velvet curtain. Kendrick stands in the doorway for a long moment, holding his breath, and then he steps inside.

"McCabe," he says, because he knows that McCabe is sitting in the chair, turned away from him, facing the window. He knows in the same way he's known all along which way to turn his feet to find this place.

There's no answer, not right away. Instead, the figure in the chair stands slowly and turns to face him.

In the waking world, Kendrick isn't a handsome man. He was once, when he was young, but a poorly-healed job of plastic surgery done to repair a face mangled by a broken bottle left him much the worse for wear. In the dreamland, though, he has greater control over his features, and he always looks as he did when he was a young man, the way he still sometimes sees himself in his own dreams.

Kendrick has never seen McCabe in the Labyrinth before, and he had never thought to ask what the other man looked like here. He's surprised to see his friend looking old, worn, tired beyond his years. His hair, which is still black in the waking world, is gray here, and wrinkles of worry mar his eyes. He looks, Kendrick thinks without being able to stop himself, like a man who might welcome death.

"I had hoped they wouldn't send you," McCabe finally says, when they're facing each other across the suddenly small room. "Though I knew they would. And, to be honest, once I failed the job myself, I needed them to, because I knew there was no one else I could trust."

Kendrick hasn't rehearsed the lines he'll say now. He's kept them out of his mind, just as he keeps everything out when he's inside the Labyrinth, everything except the thought of his quarry. "Why?" he asks, and he's surprised himself by the notes he hears in his voice, the betrayal, the hurt.

"I'm sorry," McCabe says. He doesn't step forward, he stays standing by the chair, and Kendrick can see the effort it takes him not to turn his eyes back toward the curtains. "I suppose I should have come to you first, but I wanted to spare you. I see now that I couldn't, that no matter what I did you'd have found your way here sooner or later. I wish I could have, though, that there'd been a way. Now, more than ever. Now that I know what you would do for me, how far you'd go."

Kendrick feels like he should be confused by what McCabe is saying, but it makes a strange kind of sense. McCabe learned something. Of course he did. Something that he wanted to keep secret. But men like him and Kendrick were in the business of finding secrets, of running them to the ground, even in places like this, places *made* of secrets. So he tried to hide in the one place he knew that no one, not even dream hounds, could track him: death.

"You should have told me," Kendrick says, taking a step forward. "I could have helped. I could've protected you."

McCabe shakes his head, takes a step back to match the one that Kendrick has taken forward, which makes him freeze. He's made a mistake, he realizes. He's misunderstood something.

"I'm not protecting the secret, Kendrick," McCabe says sadly, and Kendrick can see that there are tears in his eyes, this man who he's seen shot, who he's seen kill, and never seen shed a tear. "I was protecting you. But I can't, not anymore. You're here now, and even if I could make you leave without explaining, without showing you, you'd come back. Again and again, until you found out. Wouldn't you? Even if I asked you to leave it alone? Even if I asked you to walk away?"

"I'd try," Kendrick says, softly.

"But you'd fail, yes?"

A nod.

"I know. I would, too, if our places were reversed. I'd come here, eventually, to see what it was that had taken you from me. So I'll show you, I will, but you have to promise me something first."

Kendrick nods again, knowing already that he's lost somehow. Lost a friend and more than that. "Anything," Kendrick says, and McCabe tells him the secret, and then he pulls down the curtains and shows him.

**

The men guarding the two bodies are bored. It's been three hours since Kendrick plugged into the machine and dropped away from the waking world, and since then they've had nothing to do but stand and wait. There's nothing here to guard, not really, but their jobs depend on them staying, so they stay. The technician who monitors the readouts on the dozens of screens connected to Mc-Cabe and Kendrick is asleep in a chair. One of the guards stares out the big picture window, the other plays solitaire on his phone. Neither is prepared when Kendrick suddenly wakes up.

Normally, riders coming back from the Labyrinth are sluggish, half-drunk from the things they've seen, their senses still attuned to the dreamland. But Kendrick is a professional, one of the best, and he's gotten accustomed to acclimating quickly. He's on his feet before the machines can give their warning beep, and he's crossed the room before the guard has even looked up from his phone. Before the technician has come awake, Kendrick has the first guard's gun out of his shoulder holster and is using it to kill the second guard, whose phone drops to the floor and shatters. The first guard tries to elbow him, but Kendrick steps back, faster than he looks, and shoots the guard twice, once in the back and once in the side.

If the technician hadn't been asleep, he might have had time to run. Might have made it as far as the door of the hotel room. But as it is, by the time he's gathered his wits enough to be afraid, Kendrick is already standing over him, his finger already squeezing the trigger. Then he walks over to McCabe and begins unplugging machines. McCabe will die on his own, given time, without the machines to keep him alive, but there will already be more men coming, and neither of them has that much time. Kendrick touches his friend's cheek, puts the gun under his chin, and pulls the trigger.

The door of the hotel room is already locked, but he pushes a chair under the handle to slow the men who'll be coming to break it down. Then he walks over to the window and looks out and down, down all those many stories to the street below. He could do for himself the same way he did for McCabe, and he will, if he has to, but he wants a few more minutes first. He can hear the men out in the hallway already, hear their muffled shouts and the banging on the door. It won't be long until they're inside. He looks down at the gun in his hand.

Three shots are enough to shatter the window, and then he steps out. For a moment, he's flying, flying as he sometimes does in his own dreams, and then he stops dreaming for good.

***

"We're so goddamned arrogant," McCabe had said in that room in the heart of the Labyrinth. "We think we're the masters of this place, the makers of it, that it sits out here for our entertainment, our enlightenment, our edification. But we're fools, and we're wrong. That's the secret, Kendrick, just that.

"Look at this place. Look around. It doesn't seem familiar, does it? This isn't something we made with our thoughts, our wishes, our prayers. This place is a dream, of course it is, what else could it be? But it's not *our* dream." And here he had pulled down the curtain, torn it from the wall, and Kendrick had felt himself carried to the window to look out across a vast expanse, like an alien planet, with hillocks that darted at the movement of the eyes beneath, and vistas that rose and fell with gigantic breath. He had seen the great, dreaming, cyclopean thing, and he had finally understood.

AUTHOR'S NOTES:

I don't write a lot of science fiction, so when the call came to do something for *Future Lovecraft*, it took me a while to hit upon an idea. After several false starts, "The Labyrinth of Sleep" finally came together when I thought of combining Lovecraft's Dreamland stories—which I love, though they seldom get much attention, even in the Mythos-drenched world of today's weird fiction markets—with the dream-entering technology posited by movies like *Inception* and *The Cell*.

While what I set out to write was a Dreamlands story, though, the aesthetics of the titular Labyrinth and the castle at its center probably owe more to William Hope Hodgson's *House on the Borderland*—and maybe especially to Richard Corben's graphic novel adaptation of same—than to anything Lovecraft ever did.

LOVECRAFTING

"The appeal of the spectrally macabre is generally narrow because it demands from the reader a certain degree of imagination and a capacity for detachment from every-day life."
—*Supernatural Horror in Literature,* H. P. Lovecraft

I t's a scene straight from the pages of one of Gordon's earlier, more lurid stories. The graveyard scene. Dana and Conner as the latter-day resurrection men, tramping across the swampy ground in the pissing rain with a battery-powered lantern and shovels that they picked up at Home Depot.

Dana's hoodie is pulled up against the weather, her glasses spattered with drops that she can't wipe away completely because her sleeve is too damp. She wears black leggings under her jeans for warmth, but you can only tell in the places where her jeans are worn through. The shock of purple in her otherwise brown hair is hidden by the darkness and the wet.

Conner is a good foot taller than Dana, wide at the shoulders. If he were a character in a movie, he'd play basketball or football, be wearing a letter jacket. Instead, he plays chess and video games, can't stand most sports, though he's been known to do Frisbee golf on occasion. He wears a leather jacket that repels the rain, and one of the shovels is over his shoulder, while Dana carries the lantern and the other shovel. His jacket hangs unevenly due to the weight of his father's Colt .45 in his right pocket.

The lantern's light is golden and seems very small in the grave-yard, picking out just the edges of tombstones that seem to lurch out of the darkness in its uneven light, leaving everything else to shadow and rain.

DANA: Fuck Gordon for this, y'know?

From the tone of her voice, and from Conner's non-reaction, you can tell it's not the first time tonight that she's said these words.

DANA: Fuck him for leaving this to us, and fuck him for convincing us to do it in the first place. And you know what? Fuck him twice for knowing that we *would* do it.

Conner doesn't say anything, just trudges on ahead while Dana stops to wipe off her glasses again, this time taking them off and fishing under her hoodie for the edge of her relatively dry T-shirt.

DANA: He really is the Danny Ocean of this little trio, and no mistake.

CONNER: Frank Sinatra or George Clooney? Not that it matters much, I just call dibs on not being Sammy Davis Jr.

DANA: Not really any good parts for me, though I'd take Julia Roberts over Dana Phillips right about now.

CONNER: Maybe that's what the next one of those movies oughta be about. Grave robbing.

DANA: It'd be a change.

Both of them stop, the banter dead on their lips. They've come to wherever they're going, now. The lantern swings in Dana's grip, the radius of light moving up and down, revealing the inscription on the stone before them, then hiding it again. In the light the stone is fresh, smooth and unblemished, and the name on it is clear: Gordon Phillips.

CONNER: I guess this is where we start digging.

DANA: Roshambo to see who goes first?

from "The Transition of Jacob Cutter"
by Gordon Phillips

His own hands began to disturb him. When he looked at them now, he no longer saw them as hands. To him, they appeared to be something else, pincers or tendrils or things with sucking pads. The hairy claws of an ape, the digging appendages of a mole. He knew that he was wrong, that they were still just hands, and, when he concentrated, he could still see them as he knew they must look to others, but the other image was always there, superimposed, like a double exposure in an old film.

They still worked like hands, he could still grab and manipulate things with them. Before Catherine left, he could still hold her hands in his, still touch her skin, but he always knew that the other hands were lurking there, beneath the surface, itching to break free as soon as he let his guard down.

And worse, they no longer felt like his hands. Not just that he could feel their wrong texture, shaggy or squamous or chitinous or gelid, but that they never seemed like he was really in control of them. Oh, they made no overt move against him, but he still felt that it wasn't he who governed them. It was like watching the hands of your reflection in the mirror, or, closer still, watching some stranger mimic your every movement. The stranger may do everything that you do, just as you do it, but there is always the knowledge that at any moment they may stop. That thought carried with it a subtle menace, somehow more frightening than if his hands had suddenly leapt up of their own accord to strangle him.

He grew to hate his hands, and everything that he relied on them to do. He could no longer bring himself to type, and so deadlines came and went. He stopped using his phone, stopped checking his email. His computer sat dark and silent. He imagined cobwebs gathering on it. He lay in bed, curled into a ball with his hands clasped between his knees to still them, though he knew they weren't moving. He thought about movies that he'd seen with possessed hands in them, and about the carving knife in the kitchen drawer, but he never went to get it, because he knew, even then, that cutting off his hands wouldn't help.

It was in him everywhere...

A cheap-looking hotel room, two weeks earlier. Less a setting from Gordon's fiction, but maybe a crime scene in a low-budget television police drama. There's only one bed, with a confetti-colored comforter, and Conner sits on it, almost lounging, his foot hanging off, his sneaker brushing the carpet as he kicks his foot back and forth, back and forth. The light inside the room is buttery and dull, the light that creeps in from outside is cold fluorescent blue, the kind of light that makes you think of morgues in movies. That's the association that'll stick.

Dana paces in front of the big double window. The thick hotel drapes are pulled closed, but they hang slightly askew, letting the blue light in around the edges. Her circuit takes her from one taupe wall (the one with the TV and a generic painting of nightingales perched on branches) to the other taupe wall (with a matching painting, whip-poor-wills this time, and lamps screwed into the wall above the bed, casting that yellowy light). Back and forth, back and forth, like a mannequin on rails, like Conner's foot.

DANA: Why would he break into a cemetery?

It's the first time in a while either of them have spoken, they've been inhabiting their own frustrated silences, each doing their own mental pacing, but the question doesn't seem to startle the quiet. Instead it's so expected, it feels almost rhetorical.

CONNER: You know why.

DANA: Because of some stories? That doesn't make sense.

CONNER: Gordon never made a lot of sense.

DANA: More than this. Did they tell you how he got hurt?

Conner shakes his head, not long, just a brief motion, one side to the other, not interrupting the rhythm of Dana's pacing, or of his own swinging foot.

CONNER: Just that he fell, somehow, getting over the fence. A night watchman caught him, I guess, scared him off. Gordon ran, and the guy went after him. Gordon was trying to get over the fence, and then at the top, he must've just fallen. They think maybe he hit his head.

DANA: It doesn't make sense.

CONNER: It made sense to Gordon. Sense enough for him, anyway. You read his email. He was going to prove something to himself, one way or the other. If the body was there, if everything was as it was supposed to be, then great, he was wrong, he was crazy, high-strung, over-imaginative, like everybody always said. If not, if he found what I guess he was expecting to find, then he was right, at least, and he had proof. Maybe not that anybody else would buy, but maybe enough for him.

DANA: Did he actually think he could do it? Dig up a body without getting caught? Especially *that* body?

Conner is quiet, just the swishing of his shoe on the carpet. Back and forth, back and forth. It calls to mind a pendulum, a metronome, the ticking of a clock, the inevitable passage of time, the grinding approach of death. As if it's triggered by the association, the ticking of the clock on the wall becomes audible in the silence between the two friends, measuring out every beat of time that passes before Conner replies.

CONNER: I don't know what he thought. I talked to him last, what, a week ago? I drove by his place. It was a mess. Old containers of takeout food, the whole bit. Cluttered, like it got when he was working, but different too. Not just junk. He had these books. Library books, some of them, and others books from his collection, pulled down off his shelves and stacked everywhere. Lovecraft, Bierce, Poe, Machen, that lot. Biographies of them, too, collected letters.

DANA: Not unusual reading for him...

CONNER: No, but it was different, like I said. He had it all marked up, Post-it notes stuck to everything, highlighters out.

All these notes on legal pads. He must've used up half a dozen of them, all stacked next to his desk. He was working something out, working something up.

DANA: Doesn't sound all that much different than anytime he was working on a story.

CONNER: I know it doesn't, but it *was* somehow. I can't really explain it. It just *felt* different. You know in movies when they go into the room of someone who's been working out a conspiracy theory, and there's a big board with newspaper clippings and whatever else all connected up with pins and yarn? This felt like that, though not on some big board. Just, kind of all over the room.

DANA: And whatever it was he was working on, he thought he could work it out by digging up Lovecraft's body?

CONNER: He kept talking about how they all died. He had them memorized. Lovecraft dead of cancer. Poe of "congestion of the brain." Blackwood of cerebral thrombosis. Leiber of some unspecified brain disease of his own. Hodgson killed by an artillery shell in Belgium, Howard by a self-inflicted bullet to the brain, and Bierce unaccounted for somewhere in Mexico. But who knows what would have become of them had nature been left to take its course?

Dana stops pacing. She's standing by the air conditioner unit, the blue morgue light from outside catches half her face, throwing the rest into shadow.

DANA: But Gordon didn't think that's what they really died of?

Conner doesn't answer right away. He looks down at his foot, going back and forth, and he seems to become aware of the ticking of the clock, and from outside in the night the sound of cicadas, rising up suddenly. He stops moving his foot, leaves it frozen in the air, and looks up at Dana as he answers.

CONNER: No. He said that something was growing inside them.

from *"The Mimic Rout"*
by Gordon Phillips

When I venture out of my apartment now, which I do only rarely and by the gravest of necessity, I no longer see the people around me as I once did. They appear to me not as they look to each other, nor as I had always imagined them before, but as they truly are. Maimed mannequins, their crumpled faces merely pallid masks from which vacant sockets gaze.

They move with the slumping, quivering gait of broken animatronics in some sideshow spookhouse. Mindless brute creatures, their puppet strings extending unbroken into the black abyss of the heavens, toward which they cast their scripted prayers and their rote imaginings.

I always felt apart from the world, never like I belonged. I always thought that this was a defect in me, that I was a round peg in society's square hole, but now I know the truth. The other entities that inhabit this world, the others I thought of as peers and friends, coworkers and family, are in fact simple automatons, eking out a pointless existence at the behest of invisible masters they will never know or understand. The only exceptions are myself and those like me. Finally, I see us as we truly are, as well. Not the plastic flesh that we wear to blend in with the puppets, but our true forms, bulbous and many eyed, squirming and creeping and flying, sending out our own ghostly light. Each of us different, each of us truly unique, as the staggering mannequins only imagine themselves to be, but we are bound together, siblings in our difference from that mimic rout.

And when the day comes that the marionette throng sees us for what we truly are, we will seem as monstrous to them as they now seem to me. And though they are mindless things, they unconsciously abhor that which reminds them of their sameness, and so when they know us they will turn on us like the maenads who tore apart Orpheus, and, like that ancient poet, we will be rent asunder and destroyed, though even the rocks and trees refuse to strike us.

I know that this is the fate which awaits me. I see it each time I

venture out of my apartment. I see the hatred there, in their blank fac-
es on the bus and at the grocers. They hate me for my difference, even
though they don't yet know it, and one day soon they will unmake me.
    Curtains. Applause.

Dana's apartment, a month before that. A nice enough place, but small. The apartment of a student, maybe someone working her way through medical school, or law school. Light blue walls, white trim. It's dark. The only sources of illumination are the cold morgue light that comes in through the blinds, and the cone of yellow made by a small bedside lamp. A digital clock on the same bedside table says that it's three in the morning.

Dana is in bed, the phone pressed to her ear. Her glasses are off, lying on the table next to some change and her keys. It looks like maybe she got in late. There's a jacket draped over a chair at her desk, a pair of jeans in a pile on the floor next to it, though the room is otherwise neat. The dimly lit spines of the books that line her headboard aren't the kinds of things that Gordon writes. Not even a Stephen King novel to be found. Dashiell Hammett, Truman Capote, James Bond.

We can hear Gordon's voice from the other side of the line.

GORDON: Dana, listen, I'm sorry I woke you.

DANA: You said that already.

GORDON: Yeah. Look, it's just, I need someone to talk to. Need to talk to someone.

DANA: Isn't Conner around?

GORDON: He's out of town. He didn't answer. Look, I know you don't care about this stuff, but, please, Dana, just let me talk, okay?

Dana flops back onto the bed, switching the phone so that it's pressed to her other ear. She pulls the blanket up to her shoulders, closes her eyes.

DANA: Sure, bro. Go ahead and talk. I'll mumble now and then, so that you know I'm only half-asleep.

GORDON: Okay, so you're familiar with the concept of the muse, right?

DANA: "In spite of Virtue and the Muse..."

GORDON: Right, sure. But what if we've had it backward all this time? What if there's no external muse, what if instead it works the other way around?

DANA: Conner really is the better person for you to bounce story ideas off of, kid.

GORDON: This isn't a story idea. I mean, it's also that, kind of, it's been in all my stories lately, but it's just... just an *idea* idea. Just hear me out, okay?

DANA: Mmkay.

GORDON: Okay, so, what if instead of something else making us write, we're making something *by* writing. Not just making up fictional characters and worlds and whatever, but actually making something real. I mean, imagination, that's a kind of energy, right? And energy can be neither created nor destroyed.

DANA: That's matter...

GORDON: Whatever. Anyway, energy doesn't just dissipate. It goes somewhere, does something. It changes things, makes things happen, right? Imagination is a kind of radioactivity. It throws off sparks, hurls out bits of itself that get into everything around it, causes mutations. Or hell, maybe it isn't anything like science at all. Maybe it's an evocation, a magic spell. Maybe you put the right words down in the right order, and you call something up from somewhere, conjure something. Or maybe there's no difference, really, magic spell or radiation. Black mewling god at the center of the universe or the spark of creativity in the human brain. Maybe it's all one and the same.

DANA: Look, Gordy, I can't understand this kinda stuff when it *isn't* three in the morning, okay?

GORDON: I know, Dana. I just... I'm scared there's something wrong with me.

Dana smiles, though her eyes stay closed, and, when she speaks, she sounds a little more awake, a little more herself.

DANA: There's always been something wrong with you, bro. Have you talked to Dr. Sherman about this stuff?

GORDON: Yeah, a little. But it usually works better when I write it down, channel it into the work, y'know?

DANA: Or call me in the middle of the night?

GORDON: Or that, yeah.

There's a moment of silence and the sound of the connection becomes audible, a distant crackling, like tinfoil being crumpled at the bottom of a mine. Dana starts to sit up in bed again, opens her eyes. Outside, the cicadas are singing.

GORDON: Dana, I'm sorry.

DANA: Don't worry about it, kid.

But the connection has already been broken, and the phone that Dana holds in her hand is now dead.

from "The Congregation"
by Gordon Phillips

Comes now the Congregation, into this great space. They are of every shape and description, and they shine with their own inner light, like creatures of the deepest sea, like the algae that makes glowing waves upon the ocean at night, like fungus and fox fire and will-o'-the-wisps, like corpse candles and the flames of St. Elmo. They move in every way that a creature of the earth can move. They creep and scuttle, float and fly and drift and slither. Here the carapace of a crab, there the legs of a spider. Fins decorate backs, tails drag along the cold stone floors. Eye stalks waver in the darkness, and vestigial limbs grope at the air like antennae. Some are heavy and segmented, as many-legged and compound-eyed as insects. Others ooze like the cephalopod. Still others touch the ground not at all, but drift through the benighted atmosphere like jellyfish in a tidal pool. Each is different, no two the same, though they carry with them a similarity that is not of genus or of species but something else. A kinship of spirit, in the way that

*couples long married may come to resemble one another, or a pet grow
to echo its master. They are alike only in their strangeness.*

*As each one crosses in front of the altar, a momentary flicker can
be discerned, a glimpse of some other body, some other place. Boxes
buried in the ground, caged up in the dark. Not broken open, because
the creatures can pass as wraiths when needed, for they are made of
sterner stuff than the merely material world. One, a squat thing, crab-
like and knurled with knobby eyes, brings with it an image of a cave
somewhere in Mexico, and in that cave a body that is no longer truly
a body, but an empty cocoon, like the husk that a cicada leaves behind
on the bark of a tree.*

*They gather in a great circle, this eldritch congregation. Though
their speech is not the speech of men, their words not those of any
earthly language, they make themselves understood to one another.
Their ranks part open to admit another member to their gathering.
Its form is as strange as any, and its inner light glows as bright. As
it passes the altar, an image is shown of a box being lowered into the
earth, and then it creeps forward among them and is made welcome.*

The graveyard again. The lantern is sitting on Gordon's headstone near where Conner's jacket hangs, throwing its light into the
hole that Dana and Conner are digging. It is getting deep now.
Conner stands in the hole up to his shoulders, the shovel in his
hands rising and falling like the head of a pump jack as he throws
dirt onto the growing mound at the side of the grave.

Dana sits on the edge of the pit, leaning against the headstone.
The rain has stopped, and she's smoking one of Conner's cigarettes, even though she quit smoking six months ago. When she
draws on the cigarette, the molten orange glow illuminates the
lenses of her glasses, makes them opaque.

DANA: How long do you think he knew?

CONNER: That he had cancer?

Dana nods, draws on the cigarette, holds the smoke in her
mouth so long that she coughs a bit when she finally blows it out,

taking the cigarette from her lips and offering it to Conner, who wipes his wet mouth on his shirtsleeves. He takes it from her, pulls on it, and hands it back.

CONNER: He didn't think he had cancer, you know that.

DANA: So you think he really believed all that shit? That stuff in his stories, that stuff that he told us?

CONNER: You think so, too. If we didn't wonder, at least a little, we wouldn't be out here in the asshole of midnight, digging up your brother's grave.

DANA: Touché.

She stands up, brushing off the backs of her pants and taking another pull on the cigarette as she does so.

DANA: Okay, Herbert West, I think it's my turn to dig.

But before she can begin to climb down into the hole, Conner's shovel drops again, and, instead of sinking into the dirt with its usual quiet shunk, it raps like the fist of a midnight caller on the front door of Gordon's coffin. The two share a glance, Conner standing in the sucking mud at the bottom of the grave, Dana looming above him, cast in chiaroscuro by the lantern's light. In that look is the knowledge that this is the last opportunity for turning back. Dana puts her hand on the other shovel, and drops down into the damp earth at the side of the coffin. The smell is stronger now than it seemed before. Not a rotting smell, just the loamy scent of turned earth.

They work in silence, and once the lid of the casket is clear, they both stand on either side, looking down at what they've uncovered.

CONNER: This is it. Do you want to do the honors?

Dana nods mutely. She grips a shovel in both hands, opens her fingers one at a time, then closes them again the same way, like a batter stepping up to the plate.

DANA: So it's just going to be his body in here, right? He won't even be rotted much yet. He'll probably smell like an old folks' home, or something. That's all we're going to find, right?

She looks at Conner, but it's obvious that he doesn't have anything to reassure her with. He reaches up, and, from the pocket of his leather jacket, he pulls out his father's pistol.

DANA: Okay, I'm going to do it. Are you ready?

Conner nods, and Dana takes a deep breath. The casket comes open with a wrenching sound, like the lid of a crate being pried up. Conner and Dana are both breathing heavily now, almost panting. The rain has stopped. Their feet make squelching sounds as they shift in the dirt. In the trees around the graveyard, the cicadas have begun to call.

DANA: Oh shit.

The lantern tumbles from its perch above them, and the bulb shatters with a flash on the base of the headstone. Darkness rushes in behind it, and it's hard to say if there's a dim glow from the grave, or if it's just the lingering image of the light on the rods and cones of your eyes. In the dark there's a crack of thunder, maybe, or maybe it's the sound of the pistol going off. The cicadas are screaming now.

Curtains. Applause.

AUTHOR'S NOTES:

Speaking of Lovecraft, this was probably as close as I've ever come to writing a story about the Old Gent himself. I put it together for my good friend Jesse Bullington's *Letters to Lovecraft*, an anthology with a particularly unusual logline. We were asked to read over H. P. Lovecraft's seminal essay on the genre *Supernatural Horror in Literature*, choose a passage, and write a story in response.

As I was rereading *Supernatural Horror in Literature*, what stuck out to me the most was this odd streak of proto-geek pride that ran through the whole thing, with

Lovecraft's continued insistence that there was something unique and special about people who could appreciate a good supernatural tale. The seed of this story, which had already been germinating in thematically appropriate ways in my head, came to full flower from there.

With its combination of film treatment-style narration and excerpts from imaginary weird tales (sometimes with intentionally incorrect uses of obscure words), it turned out to be the strangest thing I've ever written, at least structurally, which also seems kind of appropriate.

PERSISTENCE OF VISION

I want you to act like this is all a movie. That'll make it easier.

If it was a movie, it would open with darkness. No credits, no titles, just a black screen that you stare into waiting for something to appear, waiting for the darkness to resolve into a picture. Instead, there's a voice reciting familiar words: "911, what is your emergency?"

Then another voice; a woman, crying, terrified: "There's a man in my house. He's in my bedroom."

"Are you in a safe place?"

"Now he's in the living room. He's in whatever room I go into. He's standing in the corner, pointing at me. He's talking, but I can't hear what he's saying."

At this point, you'd get the titles.

***

It wasn't the first 911 call. No one knows what the first one was. There's no way to separate it out from the others, even if anyone had wanted to. There's no way to draw the line and say, "This is the first real one. All the ones before this were just hoaxes, crazy people, misunderstandings." And then there's the question, of course, about how many of the ones before were crazy people, hoaxes? How long had it been going on, before we even knew?

And once it started, it took everyone so long to figure it out, because how do you figure something like that out? What do you do with that call, the one that played there in the dark, when the police and the EMTs arrive and find the woman crammed under her couch somehow, huddled up there like a frightened cat, dead from shock, the phone still gripped to her ear, the house otherwise deserted? What do you do with the call from a college kid who says that his fiancée went into the closet and never came out? When you look in the closet and find that it's maybe two feet square, just enough room for some clothes and the vacuum cleaner and no place for a person to go? You dismiss them, at first, of course. You take the kid into custody, notify the woman's next of kin. But after a while, there are too many. After a while, people are no longer calling 911. After a while, the phones don't work anymore, and when you pick them up all you hear is voices, hundreds of them piled atop one another, all whispering your name.

***

If this was a movie, we'd have to have some kind of song playing over the opening credits, right? Something at once unexpected and appropriate. Not Johnny Cash, because Zach Snyder's *Dawn of the Dead* remake beat us to that punch, and besides, "When the Man Comes Around" isn't quite right. So let's go just one step to the side, and get Nick Cave and company singing Dylan's "Death is Not the End."

And while the music plays, there'd be snippets of footage in the background. Stuff from security cameras, blurry cell phone videos, clips of news shows. You'd see hands coming out of a shadow where a light was just shining, showing an empty corner. You'd see a window filling with bloody handprints. You'd see a girl, being pulled into what looks like a solid wall, sliding up it, into the ceiling. Someone is running, holding the camera. The door is just a few feet away, and they look behind themselves, turning the camera with their gaze, and there's nothing behind them to be afraid of, but as they turn back the door is gone, bricked up in those few half-seconds, and then you hear a scream, and the camera goes to static.

Yeah, that's the opening credits.

***

The trick, when you're trying to compress any story into a couple of hours, is how to handle the exposition so it's not so clumsy. We'd want to avoid a text crawl or an opening narrator, because those are old-fashioned, reserved, nowadays, for more epic films, or things that purport to be "based on a true story." And while we want verisimilitude here, we also want to distance you from what's happening. That's kind of the point. Hence the song, right?

If this was an indie film, or something from overseas, we'd probably not give you any exposition at all right away. You'd just get dropped into the middle of the action, and you wouldn't have any idea what was going on. Just like in real life. Nobody knew what was happening. Most people died without ever knowing, they explained it whatever way they had to, or no way at all. There were street-corner preachers and politicians alike saying that it was God's judgment, there were cults that sprang up in the last days. There were people who were trying to give it some kind of scientific explanation, hallucinogens and black holes even as the walls were bleeding and doorknobs were disappearing under the sweaty grasps of desperate hands. Outside my window, someone had spray-painted across the side of an office building, "Now 'tis the very witching hour of night, when churchyards yawn and hell itself breathes out contagion." It seemed as good an explanation as any, at the time.

The studios wouldn't stand for that, though, so your protagonist would be someone who worked at the facility. Or maybe someone who was married to someone who worked at the facility. Someone like me.

(I'm lying to myself, of course. If Hollywood had the purse strings, we wouldn't be married, we'd be dating. And fifteen years younger. And our genders would be flipped, so that I was the one working at the facility and she was the one at home, tapping out movie reviews on her laptop in the kitchen window. We probably also wouldn't be in Montreal, but hey, maybe. They're filming more and more movies in Toronto, these days, or they were, back when they were still filming movies.)

Maybe she'd tell me about the project in the evenings, over plates of spaghetti, like she really did. Or maybe she'd keep it all secret from me, but I'd read some notes or something, after the whole thing started. One way or the other, I'd discover how they found the machine in a bricked-up basement underneath an abandoned insane asylum. (The studios would love that!) They thought it was some kind of computer, maybe one of the first computers ever built. Not really a computer at all as we know them, but something more like a difference engine. All brass and levers and numbered keys, like a cross between some kind of ancient cash register and a pipe organ. All the project was ever supposed to do was to see what this thing did, what it was. This was going to be a big break in the history of computing, but instead, it was the end of the history of anything.

They knew that something was wrong the minute they started the machine. There wasn't some slow build-up, it all happened at once. When they turned it on, there was a wave of poltergeist activity that swept out from the machine throughout the entire lab, across the river, and through all of Montreal. Every table and chair in the lab was shoved against the wall farthest from the machine. In the lunchroom a few floors up, chairs and tables overturned, plates slid off shelves to smash on the floor. Silverware magnetized. Every electronic device in the building shut down, and the entire city suffered a massive power failure.

In our apartment, all the doors slammed shut simultaneously, and the handful of VHS tapes that I still had in a box under the entertainment center all melted.

Things went to shit from there.

Following on the heels of the poltergeist activity, so close behind it that no one in the lab had even reacted, the ectoplasm began to materialize out of the valves of the machine, flowing down the sides, forming a sort of barrier around it, something that shimmered and moved almost like water. Nobody in the lab had any idea what it was then, of course, but the first one who touched it died instantly. His hair turned white, he fell to the floor choking and slapping at his chest. By the time anyone else got to him, he'd ossified, and there were hundreds of spiders crawling out of his mouth and nose.

***

In the movie version, the machine would have been the heart of everything. Its destruction would have been the end of the film, the salvation of mankind. That makes for a better ending, sends the folks in Peoria home happy. In real life, though, the machine was just the key that turned the lock. Once the door was open, there was no closing it.

They did manage to destroy the machine, eventually, and when they did, they found a corpse in the middle of it. The mummified body, hooked to thousands of copper wires, of a woman named Katrina Something, the rest of the name illegible, a powerful physical medium, born 1899, died 1916. We only know any of that, because there was a plaque on the inside of her abstract coffin that told us.

By then, the handful of people who were left from the facility had figured out sort of what the machine did. Or, at least, what it *had* done. By then, almost everyone had kind of figured it out. Everyone knew, at least, what was happening, even if a lot of them didn't give it a name. Some did, though. The Internet, when it still worked, come to our rescue, prepared to turn anything, even the end of the world, into a kind of meme. They called it the Ghost Apocalypse.

It's funny, in a way, because we had all been culturally preparing for the dead to come kill us for years by then. We just expected it to be their bodies, not their restless spirits. We had zombie apocalypse survival guides, and over on the US side of things the CDC supposedly had a disaster plan for a zombie outbreak. Nobody had a plan for ghosts, and they proved a lot harder to deal with than zombies because, frankly, nobody knew how they worked. You couldn't lay them to rest or settle their unfinished business, destroy the fetters that bound them to this mortal plane. They were pouring through now, this was their world. And you certainly couldn't just shoot them in the head. Sometimes they already didn't have a head. Sometimes they were just a voice, or a shape, or a cold draft, or the elevator door suddenly closing on you no matter what you did, and then the rest of the elevator dropping twenty-seven stories to the underground parking garage, killing everyone on board.

We only had one movie that predicted this. Well, two if you count the remake. It was *Kairo* in Japan in 2001, *Pulse* in the US in 2006, during the height of the J-horror boom, starring that girl from *Veronica Mars* and that guy from *Lost*. Well-known prognosticators of the end of the world.

(Did *Ghostbusters* and *Ghostbusters 2* predict a kind of ghost apocalypse, albeit one staved off, twice-over, by a more Hollywood-friendly happy ending? Maybe a little bit.)

It was from *Pulse* that we got the idea that saved those few of us who got saved long enough to see what a world was like populated mainly by the dead. Some kid figured it out, disseminated it on Reddit and everywhere else. After most of the power went down, people started spreading the news with hand-lettered flyers written on red paper.

It wasn't just red tape, like in the movie, though that was a great touch, guys. It was red *anything*. Something about the color red kept them out. Some people speculated it was a spectrum thing, that ghosts were some kind of light or energy themselves, and that the red spectrum disrupted them somehow. Others thought that red was the color of life, of blood and the heart and human passion. That maybe it reminded ghosts of mortality, or that it protected those who still pulsed with living blood and heat. People brave enough to do research in the big, abandoned, spooky libraries full of books that floated off the shelves or opened themselves up to thematically relevant passages, turned up records of Victorian-era "ghost traps" that were just red-painted rooms, or even containers with red interiors, designed to cage spooks.

Whatever the proof of it, it seemed to work, and so those of us who survived did so by painting the insides of everything red. Red walls, red floors, red ceilings. Painting over windows. When paint wasn't at hand, we used red paper, red markers, even red ballpoint pens, though those didn't work so well, it turned out.

From inside our red rooms we sent out parties dressed in red clothes to try to bring back food, fresh water, more paint. Most of them didn't return.

That's not a very good Hollywood ending, is it? All of us sitting in our red rooms, waiting to get picked off one by one and join the ranks of our oppressors? What they don't tell you about surviving the apocalypse is that it's really not worth it. Everyone you care about is probably dead, there's nothing fun left to do, and not a whole lot to live for. With the zombie apocalypse or whatever, at least you'd have some hope, however naïve. You could imagine a cure being found, or the zombies eventually all just rotting, if only you could outlast them. What are you supposed to do when the dead really do come back, though, and not just their carcasses? What's the endgame on *that*? They're not going to rot, get bored, go away. They're not going to sleep, or die again. There's nothing left to do, except delay the point at which they get you, a line of hopeless desperation that stretches out forever into the horizon, like a hallway in a Kubrick film.

***

I'm not going to tell you how Georgiana died. That was her name, though everyone just called her Georgie, me included. If this were a movie, you'd see it. If this were a movie, and I was the protagonist, *I* would have seen it. It would have been dramatic, would have happened at some climactic moment. I would have been there, inches away from saving her, clutching at her hand as her fingers were pulled from mine one by one. But this isn't a movie, and that's not how it happened.

I'm not going to tell you how she died, because I don't know. I wasn't there. Am I even sure that she's dead? Well, I'm pretty sure. One of her coworkers told me she was gone. Those were his words, "Georgie's gone," just before he himself was gone, pulled around a corner and just *gone*, the hallway empty for a hundred feet in both directions.

I didn't give up on her, even then. I went out looking, after the first of the red rooms got put up. In my red clothes, red hood pulled up, I went searching like I was on my way to grandmother's house. And maybe I finally found her, or she found me. I don't really know, not for sure, not anymore.

I won't tell you how she died, but I will tell you this. One last bit, and maybe it'll make for a better ending. I still go outside to smoke. How crazy is that, right? But I don't see any reason to quit anymore, and sometimes it's worth maybe being dragged down into a storm drain, or disappearing into the street, or just suddenly turning white and weeping blood. Sometimes I just want to be outside again, and there's no death horrible enough to make staying in that goddamned closed-up red room worth it for even one more minute.

On nights like that, I go out behind the building where we've been staying—it used to be a hospital, we painted up an entire wing—and I smoke a cigarette while I look out over the river. And lately, every time, I see Georgie there, standing on the edge of the water. I know that it's her, even though I can't really see her face. I'd know her in a crowd, by now, from the way she stands, the way her hair falls. I've seen her against the back of my eyelids every day since she was gone, and I'd know her backward, blindfolded. I know that it's her, and I know what she wants. Not to drag me away, not like the others, not yet. Give her time, maybe. For now, though, she just wants me to follow her. To go willingly into that good night. To grind out my cigarette and walk down into the freezing water of the St. Lawrence. And I know, as surely as I know any of this, that one night soon, I will.

Roll credits.

AUTHOR'S NOTES:

Here's another example of a sub-genre where I don't work very often: the post-apocalyptic tale. When I was asked by my frequent editor and sometime-collaborator Silvia Moreno-Garcia to be an honorary Canadian for *Fractured: Tales of the Canadian Post-Apocalypse*, I knew that I wasn't interested in any of the usual apocalyptic scenarios, so I cast about for something that would snag my attention and keep it, and I settled on the idea of a ghost apocalypse. I was inspired by the early J-horror film *Kairo* and its American remake *Pulse,* though I had actually encountered red rooms earlier, in the wonderful Terry Dowling story "The Daemon-Street Ghost Trap."

The title comes from a theory attempting to explain why a series of still images shown in rapid succession appear to move, and it always sounded so much like a description of ghostly phenomena that it's been in my notebook of possible story titles for years before I finally found the story that matched up with it.

"Persistence of Vision" has done pretty well for me, snagging me my first-ever spot in one of Ellen Datlow's genre-defining *Best Horror of the Year* volumes. I also like reading it at conventions, because it has a built-in mic drop at the end.

STRANGE BEAST

[EDITOR'S NOTE: The following manuscript has been assembled from notes left behind by Kennedy Sanchez, who was contracted with Deanna Bloom of Fetlock & Burridge to produce a book-length work entitled *Last Days on Monster Island*. The manuscript was never delivered, and Ms. Sanchez returned her advance seven days before she drowned in the swimming pool of her Tallahassee apartment complex. A subsequent police investigation ruled the drowning an accidental death. In reproducing the notes, sections printed entirely in italics indicate hand-written passages in the margins of the rest of the notes, which were printed out from her word processor and sometimes copied-and-pasted from websites. No actual manuscript for the proposed book was ever found, and the notes are presented here exactly as written.]

Deadline creeping up on me. I keep getting sidetracked, going off on tangents. I'm going to try one more time to get these into some kind of order before Deanna has my ass.

April 30, 1972 (Walpurgisnacht? Significant?) – Haruo Kitsube, Shinichi Kimura, Yoshio Amamoto, Ross Brenner, and Dereck Scott are kidnapped from a boat off the Florida coast by armed men in military fatigues and ski masks. (Ski masks even though it was a 93 degree day. It's a good detail, keep that in.) They are loaded onto *another* boat and taken to an unnamed island north of Puerto Rico (get lat/long?) where they are held at gunpoint and forced to make a movie about a giant monster.

June 21, 1972 (Summer Solstice) – After 52 days of captivity, Haruo Kitsube leaves the island in a small boat. He is picked up 5 days later (June 26) by a Coast Guard ship. He is the only person to leave the island alive. He gives one public interview about the events on the island, and otherwise remains silent on the subject until his death in 1983. There is a hearing, which is made a matter of public record in 2002.

November 3, 2011 – James Takarada, grand-nephew (great-nephew? both are correct, pick one and stick with it) of Shinichi Kimura launches a Kickstarter to fund the production of a documentary film called *Strange Beast*, intended to chronicle the bizarre ordeal that cost the life of his great-uncle.

November 27, 2011 – The Kickstarter is fully funded, securing enough to finance a trip for Takarada and his crew to the island. Just over a week later (December 6) the Kickstarter reaches a stretch goal allowing them to commission effects company Thingmaker Studios to produce an exact replica of the Zeuglodon suit from the movie.

June 5, 2012 – Takarada and his crew leave Florida on board the *Orca* bound for what the crew has dubbed "Monster Island." They plan to be there for the 40 year anniversary of the tragedy. This time, none of them will return.

IMDb Plot Summary for *Zeuglodon Attacks!* (1964): Awakened by deep-sea oil drilling, the prehistoric Zeuglodon wreaks havoc along the coast of Japan before heading toward the United States. The monster is ultimately stopped by a brave fighter pilot, a scientist, and a lovely inhabitant of the lost continent of Mu, whose people venerate the Zeuglodon and who knows the secret method of lulling it back into its thousand-year sleep. – *Written by Barugon66*

I need focus. There's so many ways I could tell this story, and I need to have a consistent approach from the word go. I want to set up the background fairly succinctly without sounding too much like I'm just exposition-dumping. The meat of the story is what happens on the island each time, but we need the background in order to understand that.

The five men who were taken from the deck of Ross Brenner's ship that sunny Sunday in April had never worked on a movie together before and, in fact, weren't working together at the time. They were actually in Florida filming two *different* movies that happened to be using some of the same locations. One was an Arnold Zenda film called *Isle of Blood* that would later be finished using different actors, while the other was a never-completed bit of Aztecsploitation (can I say that?) called *Revenge of the Jaguar God*. (See if I can get the rights to use that publicity still with the terrible Jaguar God suit that looks like it has three arms.) The men had apparently hit it off and were out on Ross Brenner's boat for a Sunday afternoon of drinking and fishing.

As near as history can tell, the kidnappers were only targeting director Haruo Kitsube, cinematographer Shinichi Kimura, and suit actor Yoshio Amamoto. The three men had previously collaborated on the 1964 film *Zeuglodon Attacks!* The kidnapping appears to have been spearheaded by Norman Cohen, a militant and what we would today call an eco-terrorist who was also a monster movie aficionado. He had seen and loved *Zeuglodon Attacks!* and wanted the three men to make a sequel from his own script called *Zeuglodon Returns*. He had even gotten hold of the original costume from the film somehow. He intended his production to be a propaganda film, expanding on the first feature's criticism of US oil interests and foreign policy.

Yeah, Kennedy, that's not exposition-y at all. ☺ See if I can track down how Cohen got his hands on the original Zeuglodon suit, since it becomes pretty central to the narrative here.

From The Dark of the Matinee Blog entry on *Zeuglodon At-tacks!:* Here's the thing about the Zeuglodon that sets it apart from pretty much every other *kaiju*: it was a real thing. Actually called a *Basilosaurus*, the name Zeuglodon was proposed by pale-ontologist Sir Richard Owen after it was discovered that the *Basi-losaurus* was really a kind of marine mammal—sort of like a pre-historic whale—and not the reptile that the *-saurus* suffix would imply. Over the years the name Zeuglodon found its way into the public imagination, thanks in part of a bunch of people discover-ing "sea serpents" that they stuck with the moniker.

The titular beast in *Zeuglodon Attacks!* looks a bit like a blue whale, but with arms and legs. There's also a row of fins or flippers down the side, which don't really match too well with the physiol-ogy of a whale, but which, being big and rubber and floppy, help disguise somewhat the suit's human occupant. Suit actor Yoshio Amamoto walked with a particular hunched-forward gait when playing the Zeuglodon, allowing these fins and the tail to drag the ground, giving the Zeuglodon's movements a particular creeping effect which still holds up remarkably well among rubber suits of the time.

Reconstructing the events on the island that preceded the first tragedy is crucial, but also difficult, as we have no records to go on except Haruo Kitsube's one brief interview, and the transcripts from the hearing. In the interview and the transcripts he called the conditions in which the filmmakers were kept "brutal," "abhor-rent," and "terrifying."

The men were kept in a cave near the shore, where they also did much of the filming. "There were guns trained on us at all times," Kitsube said in the transcripts, "and we were never alone."

Though Cohen and his men had brought them cameras and supplies, they had very little in the way of lighting or sound equip-ment, and almost nothing with which to produce special effects.

With the help of the men who were guarding them, Kitsube and the others built a miniature city in the cave, constructed primarily out of cardboard, plywood, and stacked up rocks.

"There's no way anyone could have made an actual movie in those conditions," critic Aiden Bullock said in probably the only scholarly piece written about the events on "Monster Island" prior to the launch of Takarada's Kickstarter, "and they had to have known it. That situation was always going to end in tragedy."

I need to figure out how much of the interview and transcripts I can quote in the book. Maybe Deanna can help me with that, though I'm afraid to ask.

From the only recorded interview with Haruo Kitsube after the island: "I saw them shoot [Yoshio], but there was no blood, because he was still wearing the suit. The bullets just went in and left clean black holes, like Swiss cheese. So it didn't seem real, just a bad special effect. Then he fell, down from the ledge and onto the rocks and the surf. We couldn't get to his body, they couldn't get to it, so we just left him. As I was sailing away, I could still see him there, bobbing as the waves slapped him against the rocks. But it wasn't him, it wasn't my friend, it was just the suit, the Zeuglodon, going down to sleep again in the ocean. That's how I saw him last, how I left him there."

Takarada and his crew arrived on "Monster Island" in good spirits. They had just wrapped up a very successful Kickstarter, and they were filming the movie they'd been talking about since film school. In the first video from the island—sent out as part of an update to Kickstarter backers—you can see them making land, the camera lens splattered with droplets of water. It's a rainy day, but everyone is laughing and joking as Takarada attempts to narrate, calling the island a "forbidding place." From somewhere off camera a female voice, probably belonging to boom mic operator Mackenzie

"Mack" Sheraton, intones, "It's an ugly planet. A bug planet." Ta-karada gives her a dirty look before the camera switches off.

They set up camp near the cave where the previous filmmakers were held captive. The cave is a long one that opens at one end near the beach, and then runs along the shore to some cliffs where it empties over a rocky inlet, the one where Yoshio Amamoto's body was left in the surf. Inside the cave, Takarada's crew film a startling discovery. It appears in the video footage as a sort of mirage; impossible to make out at first, slowly coalescing as the hand-held camera adjusts to light and focus, until you can see that it's the remains of the model city built by the previous filmmakers, now rendered down to rubble by time, rather than the stomping feet of the enraged Zeuglodon.

That first video, which shows the crew arriving on the island, setting up camp, and exploring the cave, is the only one that ever goes out successfully as an update to Kickstarter backers. Records indicate that the crew were left on the island with some kind of satellite array for posting Internet updates, but it appears never to have worked reliably, and that first video was uploaded by Ta-karada's partner once the ship returned to the mainland.

It ends with a shot that feels prophetic in hindsight, unaccom-panied by explanation or voiceover. The camera looks down from the cliff at the rocky inlet where Yoshio Amamoto's body was left bobbing in the surf as Haruo Kitsube sailed away. Now there is nothing to see, just smooth rocks being beaten again and again by the water.

Jesus, Kennedy, find a tone. *Are you gonna do this super-serious, or scholarly, or what? Are you reporting? Are you eulogizing? Make up your mind!*

Establish a rough timeline of events on the island. What do I have to work with? Early video, probably shot as updates to be sent to Kickstarter backers, mostly showing the crew getting ready to shoot, exploring the island. The island is small, if there weren't any plants or rocks you could probably see from one side to the other. The videos prominently feature Eugene Cullenrock, the suit actor hired to wear the repro Zeuglodon suit for the documentary. He shows up several times wearing the suit, usually without the top part on, so it's just legs and tail. Even when he wears the top part, he doesn't slouch like Amamoto did, so the flippers just kind of jump around whenever he moves. Several times in the videos he talks about how heavy the suit is, or how hot, even though it's raining in pretty much every shot.

(Is there a rainy season north of Puerto Rico in June? How do I figure that out?)

Comb through my notes, find out where it starts to really go wrong. It's somewhere in those videos. Re-watch them, look close. When is it? Where is the first indicator? Mack tells Eugene not to wear the suit when they're not filming. It's probably not supposed to go out in the backer video, would have gotten edited before the video was actually sent, but they're talking in the background of a shot Takarada is trying to get. "We don't have another one of those," she's saying, and he says something like, "I'm the one in charge of the suit," and she says, "Just don't wear it when we're not using it," and he asks what she means and she says, "I saw you when I got up to pee." He seems angry, indignant. The camera moves away after that.

The *Orca* was supposed to pick up Takarada and his crew on June 26, but when they arrived they found the camp deserted. Tents had been shredded, but most of the equipment was still intact, though some of it had been damaged by rain. Most of the rest of the information we have about what happened during those last days comes from video and audio files salvaged from that equipment.

We're getting into Weekly World News territory here, so pick a tone and stick with it. How credulous do I want to sound?

I'm transcribing the notes from my first viewing of footage recovered from one of the hand-held cameras:

Okay, we're in night vision mode now, and the camera is on the ground. Mackenzie(?) is sleeping in the foreground, or pretending to sleep, maybe, I don't know which. They're outside, but I think I can see a tent in the background. Just a big pale shape. It isn't raining for once.

(Later note added: I'm pretty sure this was Mack, trying to catch Eugene on tape walking around the camp in the Zeuglodon suit. Time stamp puts it after the argument caught on the other tape.)

How long are they going to shoot nothing?

Oh shit! Okay, that was a foot. A foot just came down in the background, but it didn't look human. It was, okay, I'm rewinding here, it was the Zeuglodon foot, absolutely. So I guess someone is walking around in the suit? There's the edges of the flippers, maybe. I wish night vision didn't make this so hard to make out. Yeah, there's the flippers, but they don't look like they did before. Why not? Is he walking different?

There's a notebook, waterproof, where Takarada kept notes on the production, mostly secret from the rest of the crew. The majority of it isn't helpful—movie stuff, written primarily in some kind of quasi-indecipherable personal shorthand, but there's something about the escalating tensions toward the end of the notebook. (What do I have to do to get permission to quote from this?)

"Eugene says he isn't using the suit at night, Mack says he is, that she's seen him. She showed him footage on her camera, and he knocked it right out of her hands. I asked him when he'd cooled down, and he said that it 'wasn't me, godammit!' I saw the footage, though, it was *someone*. And Eugene can't get into the suit by himself."

In a later entry: "Now Eugene is seeing things, too. Sounds at night, weird lights. It isn't just him and Mack, everyone has complained about something. And then, last night, when I got up to take a leak, I went outside my tent, away from camp. There were lights on in the cave, so I went to go look. I thought maybe someone had gotten up, was shooting something, or maybe I could get to the bottom of what's been making everybody crazy lately. I was sleepy, so I didn't realize until I was standing at the mouth of the cave that the lights weren't the color of any of our lights. They were blue, or maybe green, or maybe purple."

The page has been erased here, hard enough to tear through the paper and render a section illegible. The part that *can* be read starts back up: "there was something standing at the far end of the passage. I can't describe it, I'm not going to try. It was all mouth, I'll say that much, really messed up. And then it was gone."

After that, a sentence is scribbled out thoroughly enough that it can't be salvaged, and below it is written: "The boat won't be back for several more days."

From that point, Takarada's notebook becomes increasingly unreliable. Pages are torn from it, whole passages erased and re-written. The last legible words in the notebook are: "This is the end. I feel it. Everything has gone wrong."

People isolated on an island growing fractious, going crazy, disappearing, that's all fine and good. That's some Unsolved Mysteries *shit, but it's salable, as Deanna would say. I can tie in some Roanoke stuff, there's lots of opportunities to sound totally rational while also being open-ended and a little exploitative. It's these last two videos that are the problem.*

Second-to-last video:

The handheld cameras that the crew was using are time-stamped, so we can tell when things are happening. This one is June 21, starting at 11:57pm.

It's night vision again. I don't know who's holding the camera. They're leaving the camp, whoever they are, and going into the cave. They're maybe looking through the camera, because they stumble a lot, point the camera down at their feet, then back up. Down, then back up. One time when it goes down, it comes back up on what would be a jump scare in one of those found footage horror movies that are so big right now. It's Eugene, standing in the middle of what's left the miniature city on the floor of the cave. He's staring straight at whoever's holding the camera, but his eyes are glazed over. It's like he doesn't see them at all. Maybe he *has* been sleepwalking all this time.

Then there's a sound. Up til now, the video has been silent except for the hiss of the mic, the breathing of whoever's carrying the camera, the distant sound of the ocean, like from a shell held up to your ear. Now, though, there's this sound from somewhere deeper in the cave. What would I call it, in the book? A roar? A bellow? What do they call the sound that a whale makes? Songs, they call them songs, but this isn't a song, or is it? The planets in their orbits are supposed to make songs, right, and this is kind of like that? If I didn't know better, I'd think the cave itself was making the sound. And maybe it is. Rock groaning together, wind blowing through, I dunno. It sounds old, though, somehow, and it sounds hurt. So badly hurt.

The video moves past Eugene. Whoever's holding the camera doesn't talk to him. They get most of the way to the far end of the cave. There's something there. Something that's casting its own light. It's impossible to tell the color, because the night vision of the camera washes everything green, but the light doesn't seem like a lamp or a spotlight, it seems like a glow, something organic, though again, I don't know how I can tell. The camera starts to turn the corner, but then the screen pixelates out, so you can't really see what's there, just that it's big, and glowing, and making that sound that, up close now, I want to move toward, and run away from, and I'm just sitting in my apartment with my headphones plugged into my laptop.

Last video:

This one is time-stamped June 22, 2:14am.

The camera is on the floor of what I can only assume is Mackenzie's tent. She's sitting cross-legged, holding it with her feet, probably, pointing it up at her face. She's got the viewfinder turned around to face her, because she keeps looking down at it, checking to make sure that it's still watching. Night vision is off, and there's a lantern sitting somewhere off-camera, providing the only light. In its unflattering glare, we can see that she's been crying, but she's struggling not to cry now.

"Gram," she says, reading off a piece of paper that she's holding in her right hand, her eyes going to the paper, to the lens of the camera, to the viewfinder, to the wall of the tent, back to the paper. "I wrote this down, because I didn't want to get it wrong, to forget. I hope I can say it all. I hope this gets to you someday, that you get to see me, hear me."

She sniffs, her eyes continuing their circuit from paper to camera to tent and back again. "I just wanted to work on a real movie, Gram. You were so damn proud of me when I did the sound for that commercial. So proud. You taped it off the TV—who does that anymore?—and you made all your friends come over and watch it, even though I wasn't even in it, and it didn't have credits for you to see my name. You said, 'My Mackenzie recorded this,' which made it sound like I was the director or something.

"I just wanted you to have something with my name in the credits, something better than that tape you kept sitting on top of the TV for months, even after I offered to put it on a DVD for you, with a label where you'd written 'Mackenzie's commercial!'"

Mack stops, looks to the right, as though she just heard a noise, though we don't hear anything, even with the sound turned all the way up. She wipes her nose, looks at the paper, starts again. "Now I'm afraid that I won't ever see you again, and you'll never have anything with my name on it. All you'll have is this, if the guys from the boat find it, if it can get back to you somehow. Gram,

I'm sorry. I just wanted to do something you could be proud of, *really* proud of."

She takes a deep breath, maybe to steady her nerves. She closes her eyes for a minute, and the silence becomes deafening before she speaks again. "But people died here," she says. "That isn't something that goes away. I guess you know that. When Mom died, you shut up her room, even though we really didn't have the space. Even after you moved it all out, you kept everything, boxed it up. I remember you going through it. You knew, even then, that when people die, they don't go. They stick around, they leave themselves in all the things they leave behind.

"The men who died here, at least one of them, he left something behind too, I think. He was pretending to be a monster when he died, and now he's forgotten that he was ever anything else. He's turned into what he was pretending to be, and now he doesn't even know what that is anymore."

Somewhere in here, we realize that it's getting lighter outside the tent. Maybe it's dawn, but it's too early in the morning for dawn, and the color isn't quite right. Blue or green or purple, or some combination of the three. "We had a costume, you know," Mack is saying. "Like the monster the guy was pretending to be. Eugene wore it around, and he pretended to be the guy who pretended to be a monster. All that make-believe, it gets confusing, even for us. How much worse when you're dead, when nothing makes sense anymore. I don't blame him, I don't want you to blame him. I don't think it's his fault. I guess it's not our fault, either, not really. It wasn't Mom's fault that cancer got her. Death is never anyone's fault, maybe. It just comes through, and then someone is gone, and something else is there instead. A void in the shape of a person, or the shape of a suit."

The video begins to break up here, and there's a roaring, and then the tent is just gone, maybe, torn away, but it's not dark, because there's a glow coming from something. It looks like the stars, on a totally cloudless night, or like the Northern Lights, but it isn't far away, like either of those, it's right there, just beside her. And if you freeze the frame at the exact right spot, between the pixelization as the video breaks up, you can see something there.

It's translucent, but not like a ghost in an old movie. More like a jellyfish or some other deep-sea creature, and it's filled with light. It takes a lot of looking to make out the Zeuglodon suit. There's not much of it left. The mouth has grown, and split apart, and the flippers have become more like the arms of a starfish, so that now the whole thing opens up like a flower as it reaches out for Mackenzie before the video goes black.

I talked with Mackenzie's grandmother when I was first researching. She told me not to use the contents of Mackenzie's final video in the book. "Some things have trouble staying at rest," is what she said, "and it's better for all of us if we leave them that way."

She didn't want me to write the book at all, wouldn't even have let me see the video, but it was entered into evidence in the inquest, and so I was able to get a copy. You can get a lot of things when you tell people that you're writing a book. I don't know that we could ever get away with quoting it, though, and maybe that really is for the best. When I first talked to Mackenzie's grandmother, I thought she was being sentimental, or otherwise unreasonable. Now I'm starting to agree with her. And even if I do write the book, do I really want to turn it into a ghost story? Probably not. And if I did, Deanna probably wouldn't let me.

Don't kid yourself. You're writing a book about people who're dead, and every book about dead people is a ghost story, some of them just don't know it.

AUTHOR'S NOTES:

This one came about as a result of a couple of different things. From the first time I heard about the bizarre true story behind the making of the Korean giant monster film *Pulgasari*, I knew that I was going to have to use it in something somehow. The real tale—which involves a North Korean dictator kidnapping a director and forcing him to make, among other things, a giant monster movie—is one of those "truth is stranger than fiction" kinds of situations, though it fortunately has a happier ending than my version.

The other main inspiration for "Strange Beast" came from an episode of the Nigel Kneale-scripted BBC series *Beasts*, which involved a guy in a rubber monster suit suffering a psychological breakdown that begins to blur his identity with that of the monster he's playing. Put all that in a blender with my affection for *kaiju* films and ghost stories about the ghosts of unusual things (see "Nearly Human" in my previous collection) and you eventually get this story.

Written especially for this collection, I had originally intended "Strange Beast" to be a sort of modern epistolary tale, told through Kickstarter updates, Wikipedia entries, tweets, and other social media, but over the course of writing it, the format changed a bit, though some of those original elements remained in play. This is its first time in print.

PAINTED MONSTERS

"For you, the living, this mash was meant too..."
—Bobby "Boris" Pickett

Constantin Orlok was dead.

That's what the invitation told me, inside its black envelope with blue interior. It came to the family house, up in the hills, where I just happened to be staying at the time because Ronnie had kicked me out of the apartment in town again. It was addressed to my dad, so I guess Orlok's estate hadn't gotten the memo that he'd been in the ground for a little over a year. He lived just long enough to accept Granddad's posthumous Lifetime Achievement Award from the Producer's Guild. I watched his speech on YouTube.

Dad looked old and a little deflated, his hair gray at the temples in a way that I'm sure he thought made him look dignified, but actually made him look like he was cosplaying a dissolute Dr. Strange. He talked about Granddad's films as if he'd ever liked any of them, about all the big name actors and directors who'd gotten their starts working under him, or who were inspired by his lousy B-movies about giant mollusks and haunted castles. At the end of the speech, Dad talked about how proud he was to carry on his grandfather's name, and to pass it along to me. It was the last time I saw him alive.

At the funeral, he looked less like a cosplaying Dr. Strange and more like a wax effigy of John Carradine as Dracula. All the industry gossip sites listed the cause of death as "accidental overdose," but I knew that it was the colon cancer that did him in. Well, colon cancer and pride, with an able assist by Dr. Kendrick, who prescribed the pills. Dad had never been the kind of man who would meet the final credits surrounded by tubes and readouts, tended by nurses and dispassionate doctors who would see him in his weakness. He was the kind of man who wanted to look good in his coffin, and I guess he did, as good as a wax John Carradine ever could. At least he'd have been happy that the gossip sites were talking about him at all, for a change.

That just left me, and since Kirby Marsh II was in his grave out in Colma, I didn't figure anyone would mind if Kirby Marsh III opened Orlok's invitation instead. Inside the black-blue envelope was a piece of parchment paper, the message on it written by hand with a fountain pen, so that the black ink collected in tiny blotches where the writer had rested, giving the text an air of gravity. It invited my father to a party at Orlok's mansion outside Mexico City, something like a wake, a "gathering of his peers and collaborators" for the reading of his will, just like an old dark house picture. The anonymous script ended with a promise that "all debts will be paid," and included a notation saying that if the invitation's intended recipient was "no longer among the living" then his heirs or assigns would be welcome in his place.

Included in the envelope was a business card for a law firm with a made-up sounding name—Mason, Sexton, & Graves—and a URL that provided a Google maps link to Orlok's abode. Calling the RSVP number on the card rang up an automated line that knew my name before I told them, and asked me to confirm my attendance and any guests I'd be bringing along. When I hung up, I called Marla and told her to rent a car for the trip. Then, while I waited for her to show up, I distracted myself by packing so I wouldn't have to think about why I'd been so quick to accept.

It wasn't as if I'd known Orlok. To the best of my recollection, I'd never even met him, and if he owed Granddad any money, I couldn't imagine him paying up, even from beyond the grave. The fact was, I accepted because I didn't have anything better to do, no place better to go. There weren't any projects coming down the pipe with my name on them, the City of Angels left a bad taste in my mouth, and the family mansion was nothing but a bunch of too-dark halls filled with other people's memories. I knew that if I stayed there much longer I'd be making a dent in the wall of liquor that Dad kept behind the bar in the den, rather than just staring at it and salivating silently, but I wasn't ready to call Ronnie and beg his forgiveness, not just yet. So while Orlok's invitation wasn't exactly balm in Gilead, it was at least a distraction, and I didn't figure it could hurt.

Famous last words, right?

***

Marla pulled up out front in a silver Lexus, which was pretty nice, but I told her I'd have preferred a car with a little more personal style. "Cars with style get searched at border checkpoints," she replied. "And I've got two Glocks in the trunk."

Marla Crane had worked for my family for years. She didn't talk a lot about what she'd done beforehand. Dad said that she'd been in private security, working for foreign dignitaries and who-knew-what-else, but Marla called everyone she'd ever worked for before us "suits," so I couldn't be sure. What I *did* know was that Marla was the toughest SOB I'd ever met, even if she wasn't anybody's son. I'd seen her punch out a guy who must have weighed 300 pounds if he weighed an ounce, and get stabbed in the cheek with a steak knife at one of Dad's parties. She just clamped down on the blade with her teeth, broke the guy's thumb, and then proceeded to beat him unconscious before she pulled the knife out and let the EMT stitch her up. I shit you not. There was a little pale scar next to her lip that I'd point out whenever I told anyone the story.

I never asked where Dad found her in the first place, but after he stopped doing anything that required protection, I picked her up and took her with me anytime I went anyplace where I felt less than safe. I'll be the first to admit it: I'm not a tough guy. I was born into my granddad's money. I've got soft hands. I produce movies. If I'd ever wanted to work hard, I'd have become a director instead. Thankfully, I was also born without Dad's overweening pride, so I don't have anything to prove to anybody. If there's a fight, I'm happy to hunker down and let Marla take care of it. Plus, I've known her for half my life. She's kind of like having a badass big sister, and we get along.

I offered her a part in a movie one time, one of those Jason Statham-y martial arts action things that would be clogging up the video store shelves if there were any video stores anymore. She said she couldn't act, but I told her she wouldn't have to, just stand there looking tough, and then pretend to beat the shit out of a guy when the time came. She shook her head at me. "I don't play at violence," she said. "It's what my dad taught me. If you're going to hit someone, you hit them. If you're going to pull a gun, you shoot it. I'll fuck around with lots of things, but not with that. That's not for fun."

I threw my bags in the back seat—opting not to pop the trunk and check on her claim about Glocks—and dropped into the passenger side. Ostensibly that was Marla's actual job title; she was my driver. Because if you introduce someone to your driver, people are okay with that. I'm a big-shot producer, right? (Never mind that I haven't produced anything in over a year.) I'm not supposed to drive myself. Driving yourself is for commoners. But if you introduce someone to your *bodyguard*, well, that puts everything off on a bad foot right from the start. They think that you're expecting something to happen, so then *they* expect something to happen, and everything turns to shit. So driver is what it said on Marla's pay stubs, and I was happy to turn the driving over to her.

She loved driving, and could drive the hell out of any car I'd ever seen her get behind the wheel of, whereas cars and I never really got along. There, I said it, I'm a bad American.

We pulled out of the big circle driveway headed south and I watched the house recede into the Hollywood Hills. It looked like the house from the Addams Family, and it actually had purple shingles—Granddad was nothing if not a showman—and I thought, not for the first time, how disappointed he would be if he could see us now. Not just me, and not just Dad, but all of us, all of this, everything. What a crock.

***

On the drive, Marla asked where we were going, so I told her about Constantin Orlok. "That wasn't his real name, for starters, any more than Boris was Karloff's. He was from Mexico originally. They say his family came from old money, Spanish aristocracy or something, conquistador stock. I don't know when he was born, and I guess nobody else does either, because when I looked him up on IMDb, all they had were question marks. He must've been pretty old, though, because one of his first jobs was doing the monster makeup for the Spanish-language *Frankenstein*."

"There's a Spanish *Frankenstein*?"

I shook my head. "It was lost in a studio fire, but the story goes that it was shot at night after everybody else had gone home, on the same sets that James Whale used, just like the Spanish *Dracula* that same year. Sometimes people would claim to have a print of it, but I sure as hell never saw one. Just the occasional grainy still on some horror forum, claiming to be Orlok's makeup job for the monster. Always the same shot, the skin cracked and flaking, like a guy caked in mud. More golem than the stuff Jack Pierce did for Karloff. What you could see of it, anyway. Most of it was in shadow, just one eye visible, peeled open like an egg. I'll see if I can find a picture of it," as I pulled out my phone.

"I'll take your word for it," Marla said. "So how did your dad know him?"

"Dad didn't, Granddad did. Way back in his day, Orlok was a makeup man, and he was supposed to be good, like really good. Lon Chaney Senior, Man of a Thousand Faces good. What he *really* wanted to do was direct, but for some reason nobody ever let him behind a camera, not until after he got blacklisted."

"Like McCarthy blacklisted?"

"Yep, though what he got blacklisted *for* precisely depends on who you ask. Maybe he really *was* a communist, maybe he was gay, but there were other stories too, that Orlok was into some kind of cult religion, or maybe some secret society. Golden Age Hollywood stuff, people practicing secret rituals in their houses in the hills. Virgin sacrficies, that kind of thing. I remember digging through Granddad's stuff after he died and finding a particularly good bit of yellow journalism claiming that Orlok had built a chapel that was like an operating theatre, attended by the mummified corpses of dozens of rhesus monkeys."

Marla chuckled. "*Rhesus* monkeys. Shit, that's specific."

"I know, right? That's the kind of stuff that'll stick with you when you're a kid. Anyway, Hollywood was a much weirder place back then, so who knows? Whatever it was, Orlok left Hollywood in '54 and moved back to Mexico, where he produced and directed a series of increasingly bizarre horror flicks. That's where he and Granddad crossed paths. My understanding is that Granddad bought the rights to a bunch of Orlok's movies for a song, chopped 'em up, dubbed and re-edited them, and showed them on late-night TV stateside. Orlok didn't like that much, but he didn't have any legal recourse, and from what I know there was bad blood between them until Granddad died."

"Were his movies any good?"

"Orlok's? I dunno. The only one I ever saw in its original form was *The Clutching Hand*, but Granddad's chopped-up versions were, admittedly, pretty abysmal, so I don't really blame the old guy for being mad. On the other hand, if it hadn't been for Grand-dad, nobody would probably even know Orlok's name today. None of his stuff ever really got wide distribution except for that, and one of them, the one Granddad never got his hands on, is supposed to still be lost."

Marla chewed her bottom lip, thinking. "The name seems familiar."

"Orlok? It's also the name of the guy in *Nosferatu*, but yeah, there's been kind of a revival of interest in Orlok's stuff lately, thanks to the fact that you can get every damn thing on Blu-ray or VOD these days, and a couple of years back *Rue Morgue* ran a feature on him. The guy doing the writing—Gavin Somebody, or Somebody Gavin—said he'd seen the lost movie, *The Jaws of Cronus,* and that it was amazing and numinous and a bunch of other fancy words. Orlok's movies all *looked* good, I'll give them that. Granddad called him the 'Mexican Mario Bava,' and no amount of editing room butchery or bad dubbing could mess that up."

"So if Orlok and your grandpa didn't get along, why'd you get an invitation to his wake, or whatever this is?"

I shrugged, and slumped down lower in my seat. "No clue. Maybe it was some kind of deathbed remorse, wanting to repair broken bridges or something. Or maybe his estate wants to work a deal to get a bigger piece of the pie, and they're trying to play nice. That *Rue Morgue* article got some wheels spinning, I know, and Scream Factory is in talks with the lawyers to try to put Grand-dad's cuts out on Blu-ray."

Marla considered that, and for a while the only sound was the AC, and the noise of the wind and the tires on the road. "All debts will be paid, huh?"

"That's what the invitation said."

She didn't respond to that, which was just as well, because when she put it in that context, I couldn't think of any way that could be taken that sounded good.

***

While we waited at the border crossing, I used my phone to find some clips of Orlok's work so I could show them to Marla. The first was from *The Conqueror Worm*, and would have looked right at home in a Rob Zombie video, and I wouldn't swear to you that he hadn't sampled the image at some point. It was a cemetery in Mexico, that much was pretty obvious, and the graves and fallen crosses were inexplicably strewn with cobwebs. Fires burned in the distance.

A sinister-looking guy in a top hat and cape, who could have been Coffin Joe if that wasn't the wrong movie, was walking amid the graves, followed by a malformed hunchback with what looked to be particularly striking makeup, though YouTube rendered it grainy. There wasn't any sound on the clip, so we watched in silence as they stopped at a grave. Candles were burning all around it. The hunchback laid a bag down on the ground that looked like it was maybe filled with sticks, and the guy in the top hat raised his arms. The trees at the edge of the cemetery shook, and the slab started to slide away as something with too many limbs began to crawl out.

After that, I managed to find a clip that at least *claimed* to be from *The Jaws of Cronus*, and certainly didn't look familiar to me from any of Granddad's cuts. Not as visually impressive as the last one, the clip just showed a dinner party in which a bunch of nicely dressed people who all looked somewhat familiar but actually weren't—the Mexican Peter Lorre, a guy who looked exactly like Russ Tamblyn but couldn't have been, according to IMDb—sat around discussing European politics, from the sound of things. The actors were speaking in English, even though the movie had never been dubbed, as far as I was aware.

The clip opened with a heavyset gentleman channeling his very best Charles Laughton in mid-sentence, but it ended up with a dapper guy in a mustache talking about Hitler. "He was a small man," dapper mustache guy said, standing up. There was a painting on the wall behind him, but only the corner of it was in the frame, and the picture quality was too poor to really make it out. "Small and afraid. He must have felt that he was surrounded at all times by giants, and so he must always be shouting, lest they crush him."

"Who the hell uploads these things?" Marla asked, returning her attention to the road as the long line of cars ahead of us crept its way forward.

I was intrigued, though, and I pulled up the Wikipedia entry for *The Jaws of Cronus*, which I'd never bothered to look up before because, of all Orlok's movies, it was the one that didn't have anything to do with me. Skimming the plot synopsis, it appeared to involve a bunch of seemingly unrelated people gathering in a creaky old house, ostensibly for a dinner party hosted by "Colonel Ambrose," but actually for their own host of motives, most of them involving a rare painting Ambrose had smuggled out of France during World War II, which maybe explained why they were talking about Hitler.

Of course, something else also stalked those halls, something giant and unseen, and maybe related to the painting, somehow. The plot synopsis was pretty vague and a little confusing, though obviously written by a fan, comparing the movie favorably to *Malpertuis*. The only place it got into any real meat was in the last paragraph, when it talked about the movie's final scenes: *In the last moments, a hand, huge and malformed and steaming, as though freshly shaped, reaches impossibly through the open door to take the life of Ambrose, and carry him off to some unknown fate. Its bulk fills the entire doorway, only hinting at the terrible scale of the body to which it must belong.* Sounded pretty striking, I had to admit.

Most of the rest of the entry was occupied with talking about the painting that gave the movie its title and acted as the film's McGuffin. It had been painted by Orlok himself, though that fact was tagged with a notation saying "citation needed," a variation on

Goya's "Saturn Devouring His Children." But the painting, like the film, was supposed to have been lost after production. I clicked on the blue link of Orlok's name and skimmed down through his entry, looking for a summation, an ending. All I found was that *The Jaws of Cronus* had been his last film. After making it he had retired, and lived out the rest of his life in seclusion. Whoever had last updated the article didn't even seem to know that he was dead.

***

We spent the night at a Holiday Inn just a couple of hours into Mexico, in a nice suite with two beds. The next morning we drove all day again, with me dozing in the passenger seat until Marla punched me in the shoulder and pointed out the windshield at what I could only conjecture was Orlok's mansion. With the setting sun behind it turning the sky to a welter of purples and oranges, it looked like a matte painting from one of Granddad's Gothic pictures, the ones with jutting castles on wave-bitten coasts and fog-shrouded moors. I knew from the map that the ocean couldn't be too far away, but where we were all I could see was high desert. The landscape reminded me of Bronson Canyon, but this was bigger, wider, with no reminders, as there were in Griffith Park, of a metropolis waiting not far away.

The sky looked big, but not open or inviting, as the sky is supposed to look. I was reminded of a quote that I'd read somewhere, something that I couldn't quite remember, about there being another sky behind the sky, pushing it down on the earth. Or maybe I was thinking of Paul Bowles, "The sky hides the night behind it, and shelters the people beneath from the horror that lies above." They made a movie of that, didn't they? With John Malkovich?

Only I didn't feel very sheltered in that moment. I felt like the horror that lay above was right there, pressing down, as if the stars that were just coming out in the purple gloaming were bits of broken glass set in a ceiling that was slowly lowering, like that bed canopy in the Vincent Price flick. The setting sun made the shadows of even the stunted scrub brush that dotted the hillsides tall and long, and everything about the scene seemed calculated to direct the eye toward Orlok's mansion, a skull in the center of a still life.

"GPS says this is the place," Marla informed me, tapping the screen on the dash. "House of Seven Hundred Gables."

The house was suitably grand and dark, the windows all ablaze but looking small indeed against the deepening shadow of the manor. It made the family house back in the Hollywood Hills seem modest by comparison. Though Orlok's abode wasn't as grandly decorated, it made up the difference in sheer size and scope, and in the austerity of its surroundings, which lent it a grandeur that Granddad's ambitions could never have matched.

The road we were on appeared not to be a road at all but simply the drive of the great house, snaking back in the rear view long beyond where it disappeared from sight. The drive curved around a dry fountain carved with bestial fish of the sort often seen in the corners of old maps. An ancient man stood in the center, holding an arm aloft from which the hand had long since been broken, so it was impossible to fathom what he had once been presenting to the gods, whether as a sacrifice or to mock them it was impossible to tell from the blind expression on his stone face.

A valet in red livery waited to take our car. Presumably to an old coach house that had been converted into a garage, but maybe to a vast chasm with an Aztec pyramic, a la *From Dusk 'til Dawn*, who could say? Marla tossed him the keys and insisted on carrying her own bag, but I let them take mine, and we were shown into the house of Orlok. Cue the ominous music.

***

Walking through the big front doors of Orlok's mansion, I had an unusual urge: to edit Wikipedia. I felt, suddenly, that I had some

information I could offer that would make their entries on Orlok and *The Jaws of Cronus* more complete. For example, the section on the semi-famous "lost" painting from that film mentioned
that it was a variation on "Saturn Devouring his Children," but it
didn't say that in place of Goya's bestial but human-featured Saturn, Orlok's version boasted a craggy, blackened giant, its eyeless
head a moon-like mass of craters, each of them leaking some kind
of smoky light, beneath which a tusked, multi-part mouth yawned
wide. Were I updating the entry, I would have described the painting as "Goya by way of Frazetta by way of Wayne Barlowe," the
background a cloudy riot of purples and blues a hundred times
more garish than anything Goya ever committed to canvas.

Of course, the person writing the Wikipedia entry may never
even have seen the film in its entirety, and even if they had, the
movie was in black and white, so they would have had no way of
knowing about the color palette. Only someone who had walked
through Orlok's front doors could have told them that, because
the painting itself was hanging in the foyer of his mansion, given
pride of place between the two staircases that carried wine-dark
carpets and grotesquely cavorting carvings up to the second floor,
so that it was the first thing I saw when I walked in. Without
thinking too much about propriety, I snapped a picture with my
phone. That shit was going up on Instagram.

The second thing I saw was that Marla and I were hilariously
underdressed, though I took some solace in being underdressed on
purpose. While I wasn't my grandfather, I was his son's son, and I
had a certain amount of image to maintain, so while I'd brought
along a suit and a bow tie for dinner, I walked in the door wearing a Star of Hollywood shirt, in a color that my wardrobe guy
had called "neon coral," crawling with cartoonish black tarantulas.
Which, ironically, cost more than the suit I'd be changing into.

Everyone else was dressed for a dinner party or was obviously
a servant—no livery in here, nor even coats-and-tails and French
maid outfits like a spy film, but instead razor-pleated slacks, tuxedo

shirts, and black bow ties for men and women alike—and I didn't get five feet into the door before I was shaking someone's hand. A woman, blond hair gathered up into a bun and also spilling down the back of her head, some kind of complicated up-do held in place with an amber comb, something meant to appear unassuming at a glance but grow more complex the longer you looked at it. She was wearing glasses with dark rims and a skirt-suit combo in a color somewhere between blue and slate. She looked a little bit like a sexy librarian in a porno flick, but with more class. Someone you could imagine standing at the head of a board meeting. I wasn't at all surprised when she introduced herself as Ms. Mason, there on behalf of the conglomerate of lawyers who represented Orlok's estate. She knew who I was without my having to say, of course. People with the kind of money that Orlok obviously had don't hire lawyers—even posthumously—who don't do their homework thoroughly.

Once I'd been adequately glad-handed, Marla and I were passed off to one of the servers—a girl, I noticed, just enough to wonder if they were trying to manage me, and just *how* thoroughly they'd done their homework—who led us up to our rooms. We'd been given separate ones, tactfully, with an adjoining bathroom between them, the floor of it done up in black-and-white hexagonal tiles. The rooms were sumptuous, almost overly so, more like something from *Legend of Hell House* than any of the less subtle films that Granddad made. No erotic sculptures to cast suggestive shadows, though, or much in the way of ornamentation at all, save for a portrait in each room, obviously painted by the same hand that had executed the masterpiece downstairs. The one in my room was of an old man dressed in old-fashioned clothes—waistcoat and top hat, his hands folded on a cane—while the one in Marla's room showed a girl with dark hair and eyes, her skin smooth as a porcelain doll, her dress as archaic as the old man's. Both were done in a similar palette to the painting below, the flesh of the figures given an odd submarine hue of greens and blues.

Like the painting from *The Jaws of Cronus* they weren't exactly subtle, but they did have an unusual quality, what the hacks in my business sometimes called "a certain *something*." There was definitely something about them. And yes, I'd even give it to the guy from the *Rue Morgue* article, something *numinous*.

***

Since we had one bathroom to split, I showered first while Marla lay on her bed and screwed around on my tablet. Then, while she showered, I made a couple of edits to Wikipedia and looked up a tutorial video on how to tie a bow tie, since that's something I do maybe twice a year, and then went and wandered the halls of the mansion until dinner. Which, sure, was probably asking for trouble, but I figured there were enough servants around that somebody would collect me if I went anywhere I wasn't supposed to.

I didn't really have a destination in mind, but still I managed, after several dim hallways that would have been right at home in one of Granddad's Gothic pictures, to find the museum. I don't know what else you'd call it. The room was huge, bigger than any other room I'd yet seen in the mansion. I'd gone down some back set of stairs, and was now returned to the ground floor, but the ceilings of this room sailed high enough that they must have had galleys on the second floor, unilluminated windows that I could see from where I stood, hallways from which unseen observers could look down on me.

The room itself was lit by lights set into the floor, shining up on huge glass display cases that held bodies. Or, rather, the wax figures of bodies. I recognized the nearest one immediately, the Frankenstein monster with the peeled-egg eye whose picture Marla had passed on seeing. Only this was no low-res scan of a photo from an old monster magazine, this was the real deal, bigger than life. I could walk all the way around, see that the other eye wasn't a peeled egg but was instead a square slit chiseled into his granite face, like an aperture in a castle wall. I pulled out my phone to snap a picture.

Past the Frankenstein monster were other figures, some I recognized, more that I didn't. There was the top hat man I'd seen prowling the cemetery, looking much more menacing here than he had in a grainy YouTube video. At his feet was a plaque that said "COFFIN MAN." Beyond him was a giant, eight feet tall if he was an inch, looking a bit like if Rondo Hatton had gotten into some of that Teenage Mutant Ninja Turtle ooze. The displays continued to the back of the room, littered with figures that stirred half-remembered recollections from catching Granddad's mangled versions of Orlok's films, and others that stirred no memories whatsoever. All of them were sculpted with uncanny realism, work that any wax museum would be proud of, and I was aware even as I walked from one to the next in the velvet hush that I had stepped out of one tired old horror cliché and into another.

At the back of the room were two figures that differed from the rest. They were familiar too, but from someplace much more recent than my dim memories of late-night TV. A man on one side of the hall, top hat and waistcoat, a girl on the other, slight and dark of eye. The figures even retained the weird submarine coloring and undercurrents of offness from the portraits in our rooms.

I don't know how long I'd been staring when I heard the noise behind me. Not the quiet shushing of footsteps on the carpet, but a soft voice, sussurant, issuing forth a timid, "Hello?"

I turned, probably guiltily, and was faced with the dizzying sensation that I hadn't turned at all, that I was still staring ahead, up at the wax figure of the pale, dim girl. The illusion persisted only for a moment before it was broken by a host of factors: The girl before me was shorter—no, not shorter, just not up on a raised platform—and her clothes were more modern, subdued and stylish, suitable for a dinner party. Beyond that, she could have stepped down from the dais, and I resisted the urge to check behind me, to make sure that the wax figure was still where it belonged.

"Are you Kirby Marsh?" she asked. Normally that was how I introduced myself, not bothering with the III, though this time something about the circumstances and the place gave me an irrational itch to add it in. I nodded, and she introduced herself as Orlok's great-niece, saying that her name was Lenora, to which I mentally replied, "Of course it is." Out loud I said something polite, and reached out to shake the hand she offered, though she held it like she expected me to kiss it, maybe, as if she had, in fact, stepped out of some bygone era. Her skin was cold but not moist, like a statue, like stone.

"They're serving dinner, if you'll follow me," she said, and I followed, and I didn't ask her what this was all about, because really, I was beyond asking what this was all about. I had driven across half a continent; I was on this ride to the end.

***

In spite of how many people had been in the house when I walked in the front door, there were only eight place settings at dinner, counting the ones for Marla and myself. I hadn't honestly been sure whether they'd seat Marla with the rest of the guests, since she was technically "the help," but I guess when I RSVP'd her as my plus one, that was good enough for them.

Orlok's great-niece sat at the head of the table, while Ms. Mason took the foot. I was to Lenora's left, with Marla next to me, and next to her an aging ingénue who had given up trying to hide that first part. Making up the other side of the table were the kinds of people I would have imagined at this sort of thing, a heavyset man who looked uncomfortable in his tux and, next to him, an older woman with hair that was still as black as a starless night, next to that someone who could have passed as a college professor, wire glasses and a scarf around his neck giving him an air of sophistication that all the suits and tuxes in the world couldn't lend the rest of us. Marla had cleaned up sharply in a simple black dress that fit close, but that she could still move in, if the need arose.

Dinner came out in courses, and I spent my time tuning out conversation and fighting down the urge to spout some kind of non sequitur about Hitler. If there were introductions, I'd missed them, so I entertained myself by trying to guess who the other guests were, which is a lot harder in real life than it is in the movies, where you have cameras and sound cues to help you out. Knowing that Orlok had been into movies, I imagined that the rotund gentleman and the raven-haired lady were probably with the studio, while the professorial gentleman had the air of a writer or, god help us all, a critic.

Wine came around, and I asked the server, "Amontillado?" To which he gave me a blank stare, but I held my hand over the top of my glass, anyway. The server flashed a look of concern at Ms. Mason, and a crease of irritation marred her forehead—maybe they didn't like teetotalers here?—but she nodded, and the server took the bottle away. It's not easy being on the wagon at a dinner party, but I'd faced harsher crowds back in LA.

The ex-ingénue was saying something to Ms. Mason and the professorial man across from her, something that caught my attention, about masks. I gathered that she'd been in a horror movie when she was younger, some kind of slasher nonsense from the sound of it, and I cast my mind across the millions of knife-wielding maniacs I'd seen on-screen, trying to mentally smooth the wrinkles from her face and match it to a shrieking victim. "Movies like this *Scream* thing make it out like it all made so much sense," she was saying. "You see a killer in a mask and you run away. But the thing is, in those first movies, nobody ever saw the killer, not until they were getting killed too. Nobody knew to be afraid."

Pretty salient commentary for a washed-up actress. I resolved to pay more attention, but her words were starting to slur, and she was slumping to the side somewhat. Maybe she'd somehow had too much to drink already? Had dinner been going on that long? I put out my hand, even though I'd need to reach across Marla to steady the actress, if it came to that, and said, "Are you all right?" but she was already sliding out of my reach, falling to the other side of her chair. I looked around for help, but the people on the other side of the table were sliding down as well. Ms. Mason was standing up, and so was Marla, but Marla's hand was on the back of her chair for stability. The wine glass in front of her was mostly empty.

"I left my guns in the room," she was saying as she tried to right herself.

"Go," I said. "I'll be fine." Which I think I said because, that's what you say, right? I obviously wasn't going to be fine. But Marla listened, maybe because she wasn't fine either, and started to move away from the table, lurching to the sideboard. I heard the crash of a tray as a server tried to stop her—or maybe to help her—but either way she was still in good enough shape to resist that much, at least.

I stood up myself, not sure which way to run or jump, flicking my gaze around the table from one person to another. I lighted on Lenora, who was standing as well. I caught her eyes, maybe to see if she was in on this, whatever *this* was, to try to search out whether she would help. I saw something I hadn't noticed before, something that couldn't have been there before, because it's not the kind of thing you can overlook. Each of her eyes had two pupils. No, not just pupils, irises. Two of them, just touching each other, like planets in orbit. "What the fuck?" I managed to inquire, before something hit me really hard in the back of the head, and we had a scene change, just like in a movie.

***

It would have been a good transition, too. Iris out on Lenora with the freaky eyes, iris in on me waking up in Marla's bed, staring up at the painting on the wall that was Lenora's spitting image. See, Sean Pilodi at the *Village Voice*, I could *so* direct my way out of a dark room if you sent me a map and a flashlight. I struggled to sit up and felt dizzy and nauseous, like my mouth was filled with cotton. I believe I repeated the query that had gotten me hit on the head in the first place.

"You'll be fine," Marla said from somewhere across the room, unconsciously echoing the last thing I'd told her. "I checked your head, you probably don't even have a concussion. I shot that bitch whatsername, Mason, but I just got her in the shoulder. I doubt she's dead. Probably won't have much of a batting arm anymore, though."

I tried to look around, wishing I had a Coke or something, even a belt of something harder would have been fine right then, anything to take the edge off the throbbing in my head, clear the taste of fabric out of my mouth. Marla was standing a couple of paces away from the door to the room, which had a bureau pushed in front of it. Her gun was in her hand, and she was leaning on a high-backed chair. The arm that held the gun out in front of her was shaking.

"What the hell is happening?" I asked, my tongue still thick and numb.

"They drugged us," Marla said. "Who the fuck does that in real life?"

"In the wine," I said, which yeah, of course it was, but give me a break, I'd just been hit on the head.

"I made myself throw up, got the guns, came back down for you. They had you down on the floor and you were bleeding, Mason was holding some kind of curtain rod or something, I don't even know what. The servants were carrying the others away. They were wearing masks, golden masks. I think I killed one of them, I don't know. I definitely shot Mason, got you up, got you away from there. They'd taken your phone, tablet too, and my phone, all gone. Good thing I hid the guns before I left the room, or they'd be gone, too. I don't know how much longer I'm going to be able to stay upright." Even as she said it she fell into the chair, her gun still pointed at the door. "The other gun's on the floor next to the bed."

I followed where she was pointing, and there was the other Glock, as promised. I picked it up, though I hadn't shot a gun in years, didn't even know how to hold one, except what I'd seen in the movies. It felt awkward in my hand, heavy and unbalanced.

"This was a great idea," Marla said sleepily, her head lolling against the back of the chair she now sat in, her gun still pointed at the door. "I'm so glad you invited me."

Marla's eyes drifted closed, but a knock on the door pulled them back open, snapped her gun arm back up. I tried to raise my gun, too, looking at her to try to mimic how she held it. It wasn't a banging on the other side of the door, it was a simple knock, casual, courteous. The maid service, checking to see if we were ready for our linens to be changed. I heard a voice from the hall outside that I recognized as Ms. Mason's, but the professional niceties had been stripped from it. It was taunting now, sing-song. "Kirby Marsh," it turned my name into a schoolyard chant. "Come out, come out. We promise not to play so rough."

Marla had, I guess, been listening, because she squeezed the trigger abruptly, put a bullet into the door. It startled me enough that I almost fired the gun in my hand, which probably would have put a bullet in the wall or the floor. "Not very nice," that sing-song voice came from outside again. "No way for a guest to behave."

"Not very neighborly?" I shouted back, and Marla shot me a warning glare, or as much of one as she could manage. I guess my bullshit attempt at bravado saved me from, well, at best another blow on the head, because Marla's angry glance turned into a look of shock, and her gun arm swung around. I thought for a second that she was going to shoot me, which didn't make any sense, but nothing else that night made a lot of sense, so why the hell not? Maybe people with double-irises could do mind control. I'd have put that in a movie.

Whatever I thought, my brain locked gears somewhere between

"drop to the floor" and "turn around," so I did something like a pirouette and tweaked my knee, turning my right leg to jelly underneath me and spilling me into a heap on the carpet. Which fortunately put me out of the way of Marla's bullet, and still gave me a good enough window to see what she was shooting at. Something had come out of the wall, the painting above the bed swung open like a door, and just like that we were back in an old dark house movie, with me as the canary, and whatever the fuck was now crouched on the bed playing the role of the cat.

Whatever it was, it wore a golden mask, like something from an Aztec Mummy movie. Its body was human shaped, but the limbs no longer looked human. Its legs bent wrong, its arms were segmented, made up of overlapping plates that terminated in black talons. The only thing that gave its origins away were the shredded remains of pleated slacks and tuxedo shirt that still clung to it.

Marla's bullet caught it high in the chest, sent it off the far side of the bed. Even as the report rang out, the banging from outside began again, not politely this time, loud and insistent and big, the sound of a rhino throwing itself against the door. The bureau shook and shifted back a fraction of an inch.

"Shit," Marla said, as the thing behind the bed stood up again. "Go. Just go. Get the fuck out of here."

It is moments like those, or so movies would have me believe, that separate heroes from cowards. I'm sad to say that I'm still pretty thoroughly in that latter category, and it didn't take much more than Marla's shouted exhortations to make me run. My eyes shot between the door to the bathroom—bolted still from this side—and the gaping hole in the wall behind the painting. I chose the secret passage, hoping that there weren't reinforcements waiting just on the other side.

As I stepped into the space between the walls, I felt the talons of the creature in the golden mask lock around my ankle. Marla's gun went off again, and the hand let go, and I was running through the dark. I heard more gunfire behind me, the sound of splintering wood, and other noises that I couldn't identify, that I didn't *want* to identify.

There was nothing in the secret passage but dust and cobwebs, and I ran without thinking too much about where I was going. There were windows in our rooms, so that meant that the only way out would be to the right, so that's the way I went. It was dark, except for shafts of light that seemed to come from nowhere, to illuminate nothing. After a few feet I had to crawl, and then the passage sloped downward, and there were winding stairs made out of stone that I felt my way along with shaking feet, and I wondered what the hell kind of house this was, anyway.

Behind me I couldn't hear anything anymore, just my own panicked breathing echoing off the walls around me. Then the passage I was in stopped, dead-ended in darkness, and I beat myself against the wall and—I shit you not—it turned. The wall turned, and the floor turned, and on the other side it was a bookcase, I could see the edges where it had joined the rest, and I was riding a turning bookcase around into a big room filled with other bookcases and any goddamned minute now Scooby and the gang were going to show up and pull off Old Man Withers' mask and make this whole fucking fiasco make any damn sense.

My first thought was that the room on the other side of the bookcase was a library—witness all the books on the walls—but no, it was something else. A study, I guess you'd call it, or a den. Bookshelves along the walls, complete with one of those rolling ladders that I would have probably tried to hitch a ride on in less distressing circumstances, a big desk in the middle of the room, a globe on the floor. The room was dark, but there was a lamp on the desk, an antique Tiffany in heavy brass that cast just enough amber-colored light to illuminate the outlines of the place. By its glow, I could see two doors, one near the desk, one at the far end of the room. The one near the desk was closest, so I went that way.

I never even considered staying in the room. I was going to get out, get some kind of help. Somewhere in the house there'd be a phone, or I'd find my way to the front door. The valet probably still had the keys to the Lexus, but I'd walk to Mexico City if it came to that, and I'd try out my lackluster Spanish vocabulary on finding the local *policía* and, I didn't know, doing something that made any sense. I'd worry about that when I got there.

The door near the desk opened onto a much brighter room, one lit all over with dozens of candles. Candles on tall sconces, candles in elaborate candelabras, candles piled at the foot of the bizarre altar that dominated the room. The candles were every color—vivid blues and greens and purples—and they were just about the only color in a room dominated by blacks and reds. The statue above the altar seemed like it should be made of onyx, something that would swallow up the light or throw it back, but instead it was hewn out of some porous stone, something that didn't seem to interact with the light at all. I thought maybe it was some native carving, but it looked more Balinese than Mexican, its tusks reminding me of the mouth of the wannabe Saturn in Orlok's painting, and I didn't have time to look at it long anyway, because my eyes were drawn, inexorably, as in a painting, to the centerpiece of the room, the object around which all the candles were clustered, toward which they threw their light.

Compared to everything else I'd already seen that night, it was so predictable, so prosaic, that it almost wasn't frightening. Just a coffin, like other coffins I'd seen before, like the coffin Dad had lain in as they lowered him into the ground. The top part of it was open, as for a viewing, and around it were strewn white flowers. The corpse inside was dressed in an old-fashioned suit, and even without the hat he was familiar, his features had stared down at me from the portrait in my room, from the wax figure in the museum. His skin even held its odd submarine hue of greens and blues, as if in death he'd been transformed into a cartoon grotesque. I knew it was Constantin Orlok, though I'd never seen a picture of the man, not even on his Wikipedia page. I knew it as surely as if there'd been a little gold plaque below his coffin, spelling it out for me.

For several seconds, or maybe a minute, I just stood there in the candlelight, in the shadow of some unknown altar, in the company of a dead man who still felt more familiar than much of anything else I'd encountered in his house. I don't know how long I would have stayed, if nothing else had changed. Maybe that would have been where I stopped, the end of me. Maybe I wouldn't have had the strength to keep going. Maybe I would have sunk down on the floor, my back to the only door into that room, and stayed until something came for me. Until the stone monster that towered over the altar stepped down to take me. Until the candles all burned out and all I had left was darkness. I don't know, because before any of that could happen, the corpse of Constantin Orlok sat up.

He didn't sit up like a man sits up, especially an old man, as old as he would have to have been. There was no groaning, no hands on the side of the coffin for leverage, no turning onto his side. He sat up straight, his waist bending at a right angle, like half a Max Schreck in *Nosferatu*. It was enough, it was too much, and I didn't wait to see what would happen next. I went back out the door I had come in, back through the room filled with books, and out the door I hadn't tried, the door that, I found, let me back into the wax museum, through the curtains behind the two statues of Orlok and the girl who claimed to be his great-niece.

Walking past them wasn't fun, and I tried not to glance over my shoulders as I did, to see if their gazes would follow me. I was distracted anyway, my attention caught by another figure in the room, one that wasn't sculpted from wax. At the far end of the hall, barely illuminated by the lights that shone upon the Franken-stein monster, was a familiar shape, one that made my heart leap into my throat, even though I didn't know his name. The heavyset man at the dinner table, the one who'd looked uncomfortable in his tuxedo. He was standing with his back to me, his face toward the door, and he still looked uncomfortable, in fact he looked to be in pain, but he was alive and he was conscious, and maybe that meant that he'd escaped from them, as well. With two of us on the job, getting away seemed much more reasonable. Even if he was injured, at least I wasn't alone.

I said something as I walked toward him, "hey" or "hello" or something equally banal, given the circumstances, and he tried to move away from me, maybe thinking that I was one of them, and I saw that he dragged one of his legs, and I thought, yes, he must be injured after all. That was okay, though, we could help each other, and I redoubled my pace, jogging to reach him before he reached the door, though he didn't seem like he was trying for it, so much as he was just shrinking away from me. I put out my hand and grabbed his sleeve, said, "I'm sorry, but I don't know your name," and I was about to say more when he turned around.

I saw his face first, the ruined mask that it had become, the features stretched out of shape, pulled so they no longer fit. The right side sagged down, as though he'd suffered a stroke, only much, much worse. The holes in his face no longer lined up with his eyes, with his nose. Now they just looked beyond into darkness, like a mask hanging in a closet. A sound came out of the vicinity of his mouth, a groan like an ancient drawbridge, the sound that a man in a movie would make if the villain had cut out his character's tongue. That's when I looked down at my own hand, at the sleeve I held. It was ragged at the end, and at first I'd thought that he'd torn his tuxedo, but no, the tuxedo was fine, it was flesh that hung in scraps from the end of his sleeve, flesh where the single chitinous black pincer had torn through his hand to leave the fingers flapping in its wake. That pincer snipped at the air now, not directed at me, but feebly, pleadingly. The sound came from his mouth again, and I stumbled away, felt the glass of one of the display cases against my back.

There was no place to go, I realized then. No place to run. The horror in front of me, the horrors I'd left behind, it was an endless parade. I would never escape them. I could leave the house, I could leave the country, but they would never be gone. Even if I survived, I would carry them with me. Though I'm sure they were still burning in the chapel I had left behind, at that moment a gust of wind blew out all the candles in my mind, and darkness closed over me, warm and welcoming.

***

I woke for the second time that night, this time slumped in a chair in the room full of books that I had just left. I wasn't alone. I could feel other presences behind me, even without turning my head, and in the chair behind the desk across from me sat Constantin Orlok. Or rather, his corpse. It was obvious that he was dead, though his hands moved, and he looked at me. It wasn't like a man moving, like a man looking at me. It was a puppet that sat across from me, though I couldn't see what was pulling its strings.

His skin was still that pale blue-green-gray, like something floating in an aquarium, and all of his hair was white as snow. He was dressed just as he had been in the coffin, but his eyelids were open now, and what stared out at me from his sockets weren't eyes— double-irised or otherwise—but just a burning orange light, like the eyes of a pumpkin. That's actually what he reminded me of, besides a puppet; a pumpkin, hollowed out and grinning, but alive with some dancing flame inside him.

"You know why you're here?" he asked, and for anyone who ever read "The Facts in the Case of M. Valdemar," his voice was Valdemar's. Whatever you imagined Valdemar's voice to be, that sound "such as it would be madness in me to attempt describing" and to which "no similar sounds have ever jarred upon the ear of humanity." That was the voice that issued from Orlok's jaws, a voice at once harsh and grating, gelatinous and glutinous, and coming from a great distance and yet distinct and clear and easily understood.

The hideous manikin didn't continue speaking, and so I realized that he had directed the question at me, and that he expected an answer. "Because 'all debts will be paid,' is that right?" I said, managing to summon enough reserves of courage from someplace foolhardy and already broken inside of myself to answer without my voice cracking too badly.

The corpse laughed, and however awful the sound of his speaking had been, his laughter was worse. I won't even bother trying to describe it, lest I jump right over Poe and launch into the exuberantly purple histrionics of which Lovecraft is frequently accused. "Do you know what happened to my films?" Orlok asked me, thumping his gray fist on the desk. "I've read the reviews, you know, those few that there were. The speculations. That I had nothing left to say, nothing left to add to the world of cinema. Ha!"

With a jerk, Orlok's corpse stood up from his chair, and I instinctively shrank back, though he was rising only so that he could gesticulate more easily, his movements the clumsy swings of a marionette on wires. "Realism," he said, the word spit forth like something that had curdled on his tongue. "So called. That's what happened to my films. They didn't have enough vapid young people, not enough unmotivated violence. No one was afraid of them anymore. That's what he said," and here, the corpse of Orlok gestured, and I turned my head, almost unwillingly, as though I, too, were a puppet, dancing on his strings. Before I saw what he was trying to indicate, I saw Marla in the chair next to mine, her hands and ankles bound with cuffs, her head lolling unconscious. She looked alive, but she was badly torn up, bleeding from ragged wounds, her eye and cheek swelling into a purple bruise. Then my head turned further, and I looked past her, behind our chairs, at the terrible menagerie that filled the rest of the room.

I'll begin where it is easiest to begin: Ms. Mason stood in the room, her hair down and spilling over the shoulders of her suit jacket in impossibly glossy golden waves, Marla's Glock in her hand. At her side stood Lenora, still looking much as she had the last time I saw her, blissfully too far away for me to really see her eyes. Around them, though, were terrors.

The professor's glasses were gone, lost somewhere, and his head had blown up like a balloon until it popped out of his skin, revealing the slick, green-white flesh of a new head with pop-eyes and a toad's mouth. Only his scarf remained, still curled round his neck. The old woman with the black-black hair, on the other hand, had seemed to shrink into herself and to darken like a nut, so that she was lost in her own shadow, only her arms and legs jutting out, growing longer and longer, even as I watched, bending like stilts and ending in hands as long-fingered and bent as tree branches. The ingénue had kept more of her original features, one half of her face still the aging beauty, but the other had begun to melt and swirl, the eye traveling down, the teeth turning to sharp points, and her arms were covered in coarse fur, her hands like the talons of a bird.

Orlok's gesture encompassed the thing that I had seen in the Chamber of Horrors, still wearing the remnants of both the heavy-set man and his tuxedo. "The studio executive," Orlok was saying. "Is there any more loathsome a creature? For years my films made him money—yes, even in the United States, where your grandfather chopped them up to appease the masses who were already growing too jaded, too foolish to appreciate them. Then, when I completed my masterpiece, what did he tell me? 'No one wants movies like this anymore.' He called it 'quaint.' Tell me, Phillip, how quaint does it feel now?"

The mandibles of the thing that the man—Phillip, I guess—had become issued forth once again that tongueless pleading noise, the only response he could now muster. "When I realized that there was no one left who could appreciate my work," Orlok continued, "I resolved that no one would have it. I rounded up all the prints of *The Jaws of Cronus* that I could find, and I burned them. Those were the days, of course, when film was still film, and so it burned *delightfully*. But long before I was a filmmaker, I was already an artist. Do you know what it means to be an artist, Mr. Marsh? Your grandfather did, though you'd be forgiven for not knowing it, as he seemed to dedicate his whole life to covering it up."

Orlok was pacing now behind the desk, and I tried to pull my eyes back to him, because, well, a corpse was pacing and lecturing me on the Philistine nature of the modern filmgoing public—a subject on which I was probably, in actual fact, much better versed than he—and that seemed a spectacle that demanded attention, but now that I knew they were there, it was hard for me to tear my eyes from the abominations lurking behind me, even to focus on the one in front.

"An artist, Mr. Marsh, is not concerned with material success or approbation. An artist does what he does because he *must*, because of the incontrovertible dictates of the universe. Before I was anything else, I was a makeup artist, and so in my desolation, it was to my art that I once more returned. I refined my talents, in an effort to create horrors more majestic than any I had ever been able to conjure on film. Terrors that would make even those who had scoffed at me sit up and take notice. Look around yourself, Mr. Marsh. Have I succeeded?"

He didn't wait for my response, and instead continued his tirade. "However much scorn I may have for you, there is one way in which we are alike, or were. Our business was in illusion. I created makeup, masks that men could wear to let them play at being monsters. But makeup will never be enough, illusion will never suffice. No one is afraid of a painted monster, Mr. Marsh."

His voice grew quieter, more intimate, which made my stomach feel like it was trying to crawl up my throat. "So I had to go deeper. I created something more than makeup, something that could remake men as the monsters they had previously only appeared to be. You see around you the results of my handiwork. How would you judge my progress?"

Again, he seemed disinterested in any answer I could have mustered, because he didn't let my stuttering break his stride. "You probably thought you were being brought here because of the butchery that your grandfather performed on my films, didn't you?"

"It would have been my first guess," I managed, which once more elicited that godawful laugh.

"I didn't care about what Kirby did to my films," Orlok replied. "He was a weak man, obeying the dictates of his weak desires, and the inconsequential wills of his so-called audience. Do you know what your grandfather and I were to each other?"

I shook my head. "All I knew was that he bought the rights to distribute your movies in the States," I said.

"We were *brothers*," Orlok said, rounding the table, leaning perilously close to me, so that I could feel the cold that came off him, smell the scent that he carried, not of decay, but of damp stone and incalculable age. "Brothers in the art. Members of the Society of the Silver Key, filmmakers sworn to something more than just filling the coffers of the studios, from the days when Hollywood was still a land of its own, and not just a factory for producing advertisements to lull the masses. He was supposed to support me, but when I came to him, when I told him of my woes, do you know what he said to me?"

I had no idea, I'd never heard anything about this secret society or anything like it, but knowing my granddad, I could guess.

"He laughed," Orlok said, growled, snarled. "He told me that the times were changing, and that we had to change with them. 'If the people want skin and axe murders instead of castles and monsters, who're we to tell them they're wrong?' he said. *Who're we?* We're the gatekeepers, we're the masters. We're the ones who shape their nightmares, not the other way around! He had forgotten his oaths, or never meant them. He had turned his back on the Society, on me, on everything. So I waited, I perfected my art, and then, when I was finally ready, I sent for those who had wronged me. I pay my debts, Mr. Marsh. Let no man ever say that I do not."

That Orlok had more to add to his rant I have no doubt, but he didn't get the opportunity. As he paced before my chair, leaning in to underscore his points, suddenly a pair of legs whipped out and cracked into the backs of his knees, driving them out from under him. "You get caught monologuing," Marla said as Orlok's corpse crumpled to the floor in front of me, "let no man ever say that you don't."

I looked over at her, my mouth, no doubt, gaping open like that fucking Seann William Scott, and she jerked her head at me as she jumped to her feet, her ankles still chained together. "The other gun's in the alcove there," she said, and I followed her implied trajectory and saw that the entranceway with the rotating bookshelf was open, frozen in mid-turn, and that the Glock was, indeed, lying where I'd dropped it against the back of the wall. I don't know how long that moment lasted, with me rooted in place, gawping like a landed fish, before time un-froze and Marla was hefting the Tiffany lamp off the desk and bringing it down on Orlok's head and Ms. Mason was shouting something I couldn't understand and firing her gun into the back of the chair and I was running for the alcove, diving into the shadows behind the rotating bookcase, grabbing for the gun and sliding it across the floor toward Marla as the hidden door was triggered into action again, by what I don't know, and turned closed behind me, trapping me in darkness.

***

Again, I heard gunshots from the other side of the wall, and other noises that I didn't want to contemplate and can't begin to describe. For a moment I pounded against the wall, clawed at it, trying to find the trigger that would make the bookcase turn again, but then I realized that, even cuffed hand and foot, Marla was probably better off in there with me on this side. Or maybe my cowardice just finally caught up with my brain. Whatever the case, I stopped trying to activate the passage, and started feeling my way along the wall, moving along in the pitch darkness, trying to get away from the secret door before someone or something on the other side tripped it.

When I had been in the passage before, the darkness hadn't seemed so total. Maybe my panicked flight had simply blinded me to my situation—no pun intended—but now I was acutely aware of how little I could see. I don't know if you've ever been in a cave when they turned out the lights, but if not, then you've probably never been in true, total darkness. We humans are used to a little ambient light, especially in this day and age. Night lights, street lights, whatever light bleeds off our electronics and other gizmos. We never spend a moment in genuine darkness, but I did, feeling my way along that passage, and the darkness was thick, and it felt like it was getting inside of me. Crawling behind my eyes, down my throat, seeping into my joints and freezing them. Causing me to inch ahead, to flinch with each hand I put out, afraid of what I might touch.

Though there were people and monsters and god-knows-what-else just on the other side of the wall, the darkness made it feel like I was alone, like a man lost at sea, on a deserted island.

When I had come through before, I would have sworn that the passage I took led straight from the painting in Marla's room to this doorway, and as I crept away from it, I had some dim hope that I would find the way back up to Marla's room, maybe find something that would help this nightmare, if anything ever could. But I quickly realized that, though I hadn't noticed any diverting passages on my earlier trip, I wasn't retracing my steps. I was walking on a slope, and it was going down. I couldn't tell you how I knew it, since the darkness was disorienting, dizzying, made me feel how I imagine an astronaut must feel, in a capsule drifting off into the far reaches of space. Somehow, though, I could tell that I was descending.

As I went down and down, the walls under my fingers changed from wood to stone, and the stone grew cold and damp. I came to a place where the walls opened out—I could feel, somehow, that the passage I walked through had grown wider. The air here smelled like a cave, loamy and closed-up. I imagined it was what a grave would smell like, if you were inside it, and the thought did my nerves no good. I stumbled over something in the dark that rattled, and then again, and again, piles and piles of it, like dried sticks but the wrong size, and I didn't pick them up, didn't feel around, because I didn't want to feel anything that I could identify, no thank you.

Somewhere there, in the darkness below the house, in whatever catacombs existed beneath Orlok's hellish abode, I heard a voice. No, several voices. No, that's not right either, the same voice, but repeated over and over, the intonation different each time, the pitch, the tone. Like the voice of the same person, from different times, or from the same time and different universes. All saying the same thing. "He lied, he lied," the whispers told me. Under my fingers I could feel that the walls were now carved with grotesques, leering gargoyle faces and niches into which I didn't dare to reach, and I got the impression that the voices were coming from the carvings, or from the niches, or from the bones—let's stop playing coy—at my feet, or from all of the above.

"He lied," the voices said, "he said the art was his, but he lied, he lied. He wanted to make men monsters and he tried, he tried, but he failed, he failed. And here is where he cast his failures, here into the dark. And in his failure he made a deal. A deal, a deal, for it loves deals. You are not his vengeance, not that, no, you are his sacrifice, yes. But he has already sacrificed more than he knows. He is a shadow, yes, an illusion, a trick. One last illusion, in a life that was nothing else."

I wish that I had asked those voices a question. I wish that I had asked who or what they were, why they were telling me these things. I wish that I had asked them anything, but I didn't. I didn't speak at all, there in the dark, I just curled up, shrank down, and cried. I want to say wept, but I didn't even weep. Heroes weep, children cry. In that moment I was a child, afraid of the dark and everything in it, and all I could do was cry.

I don't know how long I stayed like that, crying in the dark, sur-rounded by things I couldn't even think about, but at some point

I noticed something beyond my closed eyes and the shield of my arms. A light. I opened my eyes and raised my head, and saw that I wasn't imagining it. In the distance, somewhere above me, there was a light. I wiped my nose on the sleeve of my suit, and stifled a manic laugh at the state of myself. I stood up. I didn't look at the gargoyle faces, I didn't look at the dark niches between them, I didn't look at what was scattered at my feet. I followed the light, like a will-o-the-wisp, even though I know as well as anyone where will-o-the-wisps lead.

I walked through the dark, and I found the floor sloping upward again, and I saw where the light was coming from: the ceiling was on fire. I was up high enough now that parts of the house were wood around me again, and they were burning. The house was burning. I don't know where it came from, at the time I assumed that it had sprung, fully formed, from the necessity for it. I had seen enough of Granddad's movies to know that this was how it always ended, that no matter what, whether evil was punished or evil stood victorious, at the end of the day, that big, dark house was going to burn down.

Ahead of me, a wall had fallen in, and I walked through it, past a gateway made of flames, and somehow I found myself back in the room with the altar. The coffin was still where it had stood before, and around it the candles still burned, though now the wax they burned in melted and ran as the walls around them blazed twice as brightly. Beyond the coffin, I was somehow unsurprised to see that the altar stood empty, the statue of the god or devil that had previously occupied it having now vacated its throne.

The lid of the coffin was still half-open, but the inside was no longer empty. In it was something, a shaking, quivering mass of something. Here and there remained scraps of the clothes it had previously worn in death, but nothing of the man remained, not the white hair, not the blue-gray skin. In its place was a tumorous mountain of something like coral from which jutted eye stalks and tendrils that groped feebly at the burning air. I didn't need the whispering voices to tell me what I was seeing, and my knowledge was confirmed when a familiar voice—though stripped now of all its grandeur—issued from somewhere in the pile. "It wasn't supposed to be like this," the thing that had once been Constantin Orlok moaned as I passed. I almost felt sorry for him.

The room on the other side of the door was in flames as well, the books burning on their shelves, flaming pages drifting down like snowflakes. Inhuman bodies slumped against the walls, half-consumed by fire and giving off a sickening, cooked-insect odor. Ms. Mason was among them, her flesh suit finally torn open to show something with the texture of a black pipe cleaner. Of Marla there was no sign.

Beyond the next door I was into the wax museum, where the figures were melting inside their display cases, their already-monstrous features turning to running putrescence. Here and there the glass cases lay shattered, or cracked by the heat, and I noticed that the figure of Orlok's niece was missing from the menagerie. The flames were getting hotter now, closer, and it was getting harder to breathe. I tried to remember how to get to the front door from here, how I had gotten here in my wanderings the first time. As I was passing the figure of the Frankenstein monster, I felt something like a heavy stick of butter touch my shoulder. I turned and saw that boiled-egg eye, watery and running with wax, staring at me. The monster reached at me through a hole in his glass enclosure, and looking back I saw that all the figures were pawing at their prisons with melting hands, or stumbling forward into puddles on the floor, and though it had been seemingly beyond my power before, as if I had been in a spell, I suddenly regained the ability to run.

Through the next door and then the next, and I found myself in a hallway that I had never seen before, but on the other side of it was another door, and I was rushing toward it when something arrested my progress. A hand gripped my arm, my wrist. I looked back, and saw Lenora. She looked at me with those twin-irised eyes, and she drew me close, like she had something to tell me, something to whisper, or maybe like she was going to try to kiss me, and I almost laughed at the absurdity of it all, and I opened my mouth to explain to her, even in the flames and in the madness, that I didn't swing that way, sorry, but then I saw a bead of sweat that wasn't sweat, and I jerked at my arm and it came free with her hand still fastened around my wrist as the melting wax that made up her body began to come apart. I made some kind of noise, and tried to crawl away, to crab-walk away, but I was coughing, and my head was reeling, and I realized maybe for the first time that I was breathing smoke, had been breathing it all this time, and the hallway spun around me and there was a roaring in my ears and for what felt like the millionth time that night, everything went dark.

***

The first person past tense is, as Klein once wrote, a particularly reassuring voice for a horror story. It says to you, right out of the gate, "I survived to tell the tale." So yes, let me assure you right now, I survived. What the first person past tense *doesn't* tell you is *how*, what survival meant, what you had to sacrifice to make it out the other side.

I woke looking up at the stars. The night sky that had looked so crushing and ominous before seemed wide as anything now, wide and big and welcoming. Nothing else mattered, except that I was looking up at the sky. The burning in my lungs, the scraped raw feeling in my throat, the aching in my joints. None of it was worth a tinker's damn in the face of that knowledge, that there was no ceiling above me—whether burning or otherwise—that I was outside. Outside, I could face anything.

I sat up and looked over at Marla, who was sitting on a rock next to me. In the moonlight, all of her blood looked like chocolate syrup, and there was so, so much of it. "The garage burned too," was the first thing she said to me, and I turned my head the other direction and saw it, like a campfire turned up to eleven, the mansion still blazing, all of it going up, just like in one of Granddad's movies.

"At least it was a rental," I said, the punch line broken by a cough. There were tears on my cheeks, though whether from relief or still left over from the smoke, I couldn't say. I started to ask Marla how she was doing, if she was okay, but when I went to speak instead I heard a barking. Not from my throat, but from the direction of the house. Once, twice, and again. Confused, I looked at Marla, and saw her crumple to the sandy dirt. Ragged blooms had appeared in her chest, leaking chocolate syrup. I turned back as I heard a firing pin click on an empty chamber, and I saw a shadow taking shape from the dancing heat of the flames. I imagined the statue from the altar, striding about like the giant in *The Jaws of Cronus*, ready to reach out and pluck me from the edge of my perceived salvation and drag me back into the flames, like the ending of some *conte cruel*. But it wasn't the statue. It was small and slight and dark, and it held Marla's other Glock shining silver in the firelight, though as I watched it tossed the gun away, into the dirt.

Its eyes glowed with an unwholesome luminescence, save for the twin moons of the doubled irises, and I knew that this one wasn't wax. "What the hell do you want?" I asked it, as it drew nearer. "What the hell is left?"

"Hell has nothing to do with it," it said, and its voice was nothing dramatic, as Orlok's had been. Just the voice of a girl, small and slight, though no longer demure, no longer unassuming, and I realized that there had probably never been a Lenora, that it had probably always been this. "Desperation is what I want. Desperate men make deals, and deals are what I crave. Orlok came to me with his desperation, shouted it into the darkness and I answered. What is it that you are desperate for, Kirby Marsh?"

I want to say that I spat on it, but I couldn't. My mouth was filled with ashes.

"Your friend doesn't have to die out here, you know," it said. "You don't have to die. This," and it gestured to take in the burning house, the moonlit desert, the sheltering sky, "doesn't have to be the last thing you see before the credits roll. There can be a trade. There can always be a trade."

I looked down, and saw that Marla had crawled back onto her hands and knees, but I could also see that her shadow was bigger than it should have been, and it glistened in the light from the fire. The look in her eyes told me that she was out of bullets, and the rest of her told me that she was almost out of blood, out of time. She reached out and gripped my hand, and in spite of everything hers was steady, while mine shook. She looked me in the eye, and she said six magic words:

"You always were an asshole, Gorman."

***

That's where I should leave you. It's the better ending, the top still spinning, MacReady and Childs sitting in the cold. It gives you ambiguity, and it gives you hope. But it's another illusion, a false front, a mask. The ambiguity is a lie, and so is the hope.

It would make for a better ending if we had one bullet left, one last trick, but neither of us did. We were alone and we were broken and all that we had was the desert and the fathomless dark up above us. And even if there had been a bullet, a stick of dynamite, a grenade with no pin, the thing with the doubled irises wasn't something that you can fight that way; it wasn't something that you fight at all. It was the other sky that the sky hides behind it, the terror that lies above, and below, and in the howling gulf that is on every side of this moment.

So I made the deal, because that's what you do when everything else is gone. And while I can't leave you with ambiguity, and I can't leave you with hope, I can leave you with this: I may not be my granddad, but I am his son's son, and while I may not be an artist, I am a movie producer, and I made a better deal than Orlok did.

AUTHOR'S NOTES:

The first place I ever encountered the quote that serves as the epigram for this book and gives this story its title was in Jason Zinoman's book *Shock Value*. From there, I was compelled to track down the 1968 Peter Bogdanovich film *Targets*, which to me provided an almost perfect summary of the change in horror films from the '60s to the '70s, not only in what we gained in the transition, but also in what we lost. That transition, and the nostalgic longing captured in the quote, gave me not only the idea for this story, but also the central theme of this entire collection.

While most of the other stories in this collection are inspired by horror movies, or touch upon particular periods in the history of horror film, this story is intended as sort of whirlwind ride across horror's cinematic history, thanks in part to the multi-generational family of horror producers that culminate in Kirby Marsh III. This absolutely isn't the last time you'll see the Marsh family show up in my stories, and in fact our protagonist's grandfather has already appeared in something else I did; a fragment that I wrote as part of a special project for Michael Bukowski's Yog-Blogsoth website.

"Painted Monsters" is perhaps more packed with references and inspirations than anything else I've ever written, and if I took the time to list them all, I'd be writing a missive as long as the story itself. This was my chance to play in a lot of my favorite sandboxes all at the same time, and as a result, I think it's one of the most "me" things I've ever done. Like the majority of my stories, it owes a big debt to Mike Mignola, though this time it's less in the content, I think, than in the style of plotting I employed. I hope that the beats of this story would feel right at home in a Hellboy comic, though Hellboy would have handled the situation very differently than poor, passive Kirby Marsh III.

AFTERWORD & ACKNOWLEDGMENTS

I watch a lot of movies. If you read through the rest of the book before getting here, that probably doesn't come as much of a surprise. While I was working on assembling the manuscript for this collection, I happened to watch the 1988 Anthony Hickox film *Waxwork* and noticed that it was dedicated to: "Hammer, Argento, Romero, Dante, Landis, Spielberg, Wells, Carpenter, Mum and Dad, and many more…" That could easily have been the dedication for this book, if I hadn't already settled on the one that you saw at the front.

Movies have always worked themselves into my imagination and my stories in a lot of ways, some that I'm probably not even aware of. I think a couple of early experiences with horror movies shaped my storytelling pretty profoundly. One I already talked about in the author's notes of "The Murders on Morgue Street," paging through books full of evocative, black-and-white stills from old monster movies and trying to imagine the movie in my head. The other is that, when I was a kid, we got a local station that showed monster movies—complete with a horror host, unless my memory is playing tricks on me—on Saturday mornings. So when other kids my age were watching cartoons, I watched *Squirm* and *Willard* and *The Food of the Gods* and about a jillion Godzilla movies.

When I started assembling this collection, I knew that it was going to consist almost entirely of stories that dealt with cinema, either head-on or obliquely. I already had the quote from *Targets* chosen as my epigram, and I knew that I wanted to take the reader through a kind of exploration of the ways that horror—especially in movies—had changed over the years. So the earliest stories in this book are inspired by silent horror films and the black-and-white monster movies of the '30s, while we gradually make our way through *Gialli* and many others before winding up in the present day, with found footage and self-awareness and the ubiquity of movies about ghosts. And then there's the closing novelette, which is a kind of microcosm of the rest of the book, pulling in influences from every era of horror cinema into one big monster mash.

While putting the table of contents together, though, another theme appeared to me, one that I hadn't expected. Call it "Death, and What Comes After." Not necessarily in the form of an afterlife, per se, but in the legacies, mysteries, and regrets that are left behind when someone passes away. In virtually every story in this collection there has been a death—or, in a couple of cases, something very *like* a death—and the protagonists are those who remain behind, dealing with the fallout.

This wasn't the result of any conscious decision on my part. It wasn't even something I noticed until I had all the stories gathered in one place. But it permeates just about every story that I wrote during this period. Maybe it's because my wife had lost someone very close to her before the earliest of these stories were written, and she lost another family member as the collection was nearing completion. Or maybe it's because my own father, with whom I've never had an easy relationship, was teetering on the brink during the writing of most of these stories, and he finally passed away just after I finished the first draft of this manuscript.

I've never been someone who was much troubled by the thought of my own mortality, but seeing the impact of death—or its imminence—on those who remain behind left an indelible mark on me and my fiction.

***

I sold this collection to Ross Lockhart's Word Horde imprint at the 2014 H.P. Lovecraft Film Festival in Portland, which seems appropriate. When it comes time to thank people for their role in helping to usher this book into existence, he'll have to be at the top of my list. He's been a vocal champion of my work ever since "Black Hill" (from my previous collection) first appeared in *The Book of Cthulhu 2*, and not only is he the publisher for this volume, but he also previously published three of the stories contained herein.

I also need to extend my gratitude to John Langan for his introduction, and to Nick Gucker for taking on the art duties, as well as everyone who read this collection or any of these stories in manuscript form and provided feedback, blurbs, or simple enthusiasm and moral support.

Writing is often a lonely occupation, but the fact of the matter is that an inordinate number of people go into helping a book make it from conception to print. There's no way I could ever thank everyone who deserves it, but I'd be hugely remiss not to mention a few. Thanks to Jeff Owens for giving me the job at the video store where I worked through the end of college and a little beyond, and to Tim Canton, Silvia Moreno-Garcia, and Paula Stiles for providing forums for me to occasionally ramble about horror movies. Thanks to Jay, Steve, Bear, Jeremy, Sean, and Jason, for not only being my friends and talking shop, but for watching more ridiculous movies with me than probably anyone else around. And thanks of course to my eternally supportive wife Grace, who may not share my affection for bad monster movies, but has seemingly infinite patience for me and my obsessions.

I've been extremely lucky as a writer and have gotten to work with a lot of really great people over the years, so thanks also to everyone who originally published one of the stories in this collection—or anything else I've ever done. Thanks to the guys at Valancourt Books, and to everybody at Privateer Press, current and past, most especially Simon, Aeryn, Mike, Matt, Darla, and Doug.

Finally, thanks to anyone and everyone who ever made a crappy monster movie—or who sat through one with me—without you guys, I'd just be sitting alone in the dark. And last of all, before those final credits roll, thanks to you, dear eternal reader. Be sure to dim the lights before the next feature starts.

TITLES AVAILABLE FROM WORD HORDE

Tales of Jack the Ripper
an anthology edited by Ross E. Lockhart

We Leave Together
a Dogsland novel by J. M. McDermott

*The Children of Old Leech: A Tribute to the
Carnivorous Cosmos of Laird Barron*
an anthology edited by Ross E. Lockhart and Justin Steele

Vermilion
a novel by Molly Tanzer

Giallo Fantastique
an anthology edited by Ross E. Lockhart

Mr. Suicide
a novel by Nicole Cushing

Cthulhu Fhtagn!
an anthology edited by Ross E. Lockhart

Painted Monsters
a collection by Orrin Grey

Furnace: Stories (February 2016)
a collection by Livia Llewellyn

Ask for Word Horde books by name at your favorite bookseller.

Or order online at www.WordHorde.com

"A lavish, sumptuous tapestry of luxurious surrealism and strangeness."

—*The Horror Fiction Review*

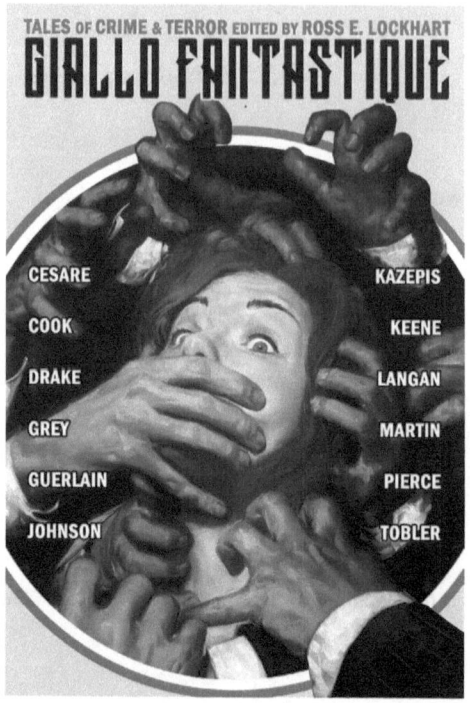

AN ANTHOLOGY OF ORIGINAL STRANGE STORIES
at the intersection of crime, terror, and supernatural fiction.
Inspired by and drawing from the highly stylized cinematic
thrillers of Argento, Bava, and Fulci; American noir and crime
fiction; and the grim fantasies of Edgar Allan Poe, Guy de
Maupassant, and Jean Ray, *Giallo Fantastique* seeks to unnerve
readers through virtuoso storytelling and startlingly colorful
imagery.

What's your favorite shade of yellow?

Trade Paperback, 240 pp, $15.99
ISBN-13: 978-1-939905-06-2
http://www.wordhorde.com

In his house at R'lyeh, Cthulhu waits dreaming…

WHAT ARE THE DREAMS THAT MONSTERS DREAM?
When will the stars grow right? Where are the sunken temples
in which the dreamers dwell? How will it all change when they
come home?

Within these pages lie the answers, and more, in all-new stories
by many of the brightest lights in dark fiction. Gathered
together by Ross E. Lockhart, the editor who brought you
The Book of Cthulhu, *The Children of Old Leech*, and *Giallo
Fantastique*, *Cthulhu Fhtagn!* features nineteen weird tales
inspired by H. P. Lovecraft.

Format: Trade Paperback, 324 pp, $19.99
ISBN-13: 978-1-939905-13-0
http://www.wordhorde.com

ABOUT THE AUTHOR:

O rrin Grey is a skeleton who likes monsters, as well as a writer, editor, and amateur film scholar who was born on the night before Halloween. *Painted Monsters* is his second collection of weird stories. His writing on film has appeared in places like *Strange Horizons* and *Clarkesworld*, and he writes a regular column on vintage horror cinema for *Innsmouth Free Press*. You can find him online at orringrey.com.